Danny Dunn and the Anti-gravity Paint

DANNY DUNN

and the

Anti - gravity Paint

by Jay Williams & Raymond Abrashkin

Illustrated by Ezra Jack Keats

McGRAW-HILL BOOK COMPANY

NEW YORK   TORONTO   LONDON

Also by Jay Williams and Raymond Abrashkin

DANNY DUNN AND THE
AUTOMATIC HOUSE
DANNY DUNN AND THE FOSSIL CAVE
DANNY DUNN AND THE HEAT RAY
DANNY DUNN AND THE
HOMEWORK MACHINE
DANNY DUNN, TIME TRAVELER
DANNY DUNN AND THE
WEATHER MACHINE
DANNY DUNN ON A DESERT ISLAND
DANNY DUNN ON THE OCEAN FLOOR

*For Hank and John
and Chris and Vickie*

Contents

Danny Dunn and the Anti-gravity Paint

CHAPTER ONE

"I Will Not Daydream . . ."

Space Captain Daniel Dunn stood on the bridge of the *Revenge* with his eyes on the viewer screens. He could see the fiery trails that were the rocket ships from Jupiter.

Adjutant Dan Dunn ran up to report. "Sir," he cried, "they've got us surrounded!"

"We'll fight 'em all, singlehanded," said the Captain, his handsome, lined face hardening with decision. He turned to the pilot. "Grid 4-X67!" he barked. "Get set, Dan, and blast away!"

Pilot Danny Dunn glanced at his instruments. He pressed down the firing lever.

At that instant one of the Jovian ships darted in close, her bow guns sparkling. Jets of power smashed against the side of the *Revenge*. She rocked and swung. Pilot Dunn was thrown from side to side, but his finger never left the firing lever.

"We'll ram them!" Captain Dunn cried. He

seized the controls and swung the ship directly at the nearest enemy vessel.

CRASH! The impact knocked him off his feet. Everything went black.

"Daniel Dunn! What on earth do you think you're doing?"

The voice was that of his teacher, Miss Arnold.

Danny found himself sitting on the floor of his classroom. The rocket-ship control panel vanished. So did the enemy ships. Danny's eyes cleared, and he looked up at Miss Arnold's face, with its sharp brown eyes that seemed to pierce right through him.

"Uh—nothing, Miss Arnold," he mumbled.

"Nothing!" The teacher put her hands on her hips. "Do you call groaning and moaning and falling flat on the floor 'nothing'? Don't you feel well? Speak up, boy!"

"No, ma'am. I mean, sure, I feel fine," Danny stammered.

Miss Arnold raised one eyebrow. "Get back in your seat," she said. "You certainly weren't doing arithmetic." Her voice softened. "What *were* you doing?"

Danny got to his feet and dusted himself off. He could see Eddie Philips hiding a grin behind his hand. Fat Carver rolled his eyes at the ceiling and pretended to whistle. Most of the other boys and girls were giggling. Only his best friend, Joe Pearson, was looking at him sadly.

He sat down. Miss Arnold repeated, "Well? I'm waiting."

"I—I was thinking," he said at last.

"Thinking?"

"Yes'm."

"Are you in the habit of falling down when you think?"

The class laughed. Danny felt his face redden.

Eddie Philips, nicknamed "Snitcher," raised his hand. "I bet I can tell you where he was, Miss Arnold. He was in a rocket ship. He's always playing something like that."

Danny shot a fierce glance at Eddie.

Miss Arnold's face twitched. She almost smiled, but bit her lip instead. "Is that true, Danny?"

He nodded sullenly.

"Hm." She went back to her desk. "Now look here, Dan. I know how hard it is for plain, old-fashioned arithmetic to stand up to rocket ships. But let's remember that trips to Mars are far in the future. It will be a long time before anything like that happens. Meantime, I suggest you stick to the present."

"Yes, ma'am," said Danny. Then he added, "But Professor Bullfinch says that space travel may come in the next ten years."

"I know all about Professor Bullfinch," said Miss Arnold firmly, "and I have a great deal of respect for him. But if you don't make better marks in arithmetic, *you'll* never become a scientist."

"Well, gee, Miss Arnold," Danny objected, "what about Einstein? He flunked arithmetic."

Miss Arnold's lips tightened. "Danny," she said, "I don't want to hear any more about it. I must think of some way of keeping you on earth." She thought for a moment, and then she said, "It's not as if this were the first time. Since nothing else seems to work, perhaps we'd better try an old-fashioned punishment. I want you to write a hundred times, 'I will not daydream about space flight in class.' Let me see it tomorrow morning."

She stood up and went to the blackboard. Danny, with a sigh, pulled his mind away from the exciting mysteries of outer space and went back to fractions.

When school was over, he walked home with Joe Pearson. Joe was his own age, but where Danny was stocky and red-haired, Joe was thin

and dark, with a face that was always mournful, no matter how happy he was.

"Gosh, that's tough, Danny," Joe said. "Having to do all those sentences, I mean."

"I don't care," said Danny. "But she was wrong. Professor Bullfinch told me that space flight is just around the corner."

Joe shook his head. "Yeah. But maybe you ought to keep away from science for a while. It never brings you anything but trouble. Remember when you were trying to build your own dynamo? You dammed up the culvert on Breakneck Hill for water power and flooded all the cellars of the houses up there."

Danny grunted. "That was an accident."

"And the time in Mr. Winkle's science class when you poured all his chemicals into one jar to see what would happen? That was no accident.

Ooh, golly, that smell, when I think of it, it just makes me seasick."

"Well, that was last year. I was only a kid then," Danny said. "But that's got nothing to do with space flight."

"You'll just blow us all up," Joe said, his voice getting gloomier than ever.

"Oh, come on, Joe," Danny said to his friend. "You're always looking on the dark side." He jammed his hands into his pockets. "You'll see. One of these days I'll be on that first rocket ship heading for the Moon. A long time in the future! Ha! Did you read about the satellite they sent up yesterday?"

"That thing that's supposed to circle the earth?"

"Yes. It'll soar from two to fourteen hundred miles above the earth, and it travels about eighteen thousand miles an hour!"

"If it keeps going round and round the earth, what good is it?" Joe asked. "It never goes anywhere."

"It's not supposed to go anywhere."

"Then what's the good of it? I mean, if you're going as fast as eighteen thousand miles an hour, you should get somewhere else instead of just—"

"It doesn't have to get anywhere," Danny explained. "It's supposed to circle the earth and send back information about cosmic rays and meteors and things like that. It's the first step, Joe! Next they can build a space station, and then, after that, rocket flights into space." His eyes shone.

But Joe just shook his head. "Trouble," he said. "That's all there'll be."

They came to Dan's house. Danny said good-by to his friend. In spite of his jaunty manner with Joe, he felt anything but cheerful once he had closed the front door behind him. For all he could think of was a hundred sentences stretching out over the next few hours—long sentences, too.

CHAPTER TWO

The Satellite

Danny's mother was housekeeper for Professor Euclid Bullfinch. When Danny was no more than a baby, her husband had died and she had been forced to find work and a home for her infant son. Professor Bullfinch taught at Midston University. But his reputation was nationwide. He had invented a number of scientific devices that brought him enough money so that he could keep up his own laboratory and do independent research. He lived alone and needed someone to cook and keep house for him.

Danny had grown up under the Professor's roof and was full of affection for the quiet, thoughtful scientist. He was determined to become as much like him as he could. The Professor not only took the place of the father Danny had never known, but had become his friend as well.

Each day after school Danny spent some time with the Professor. Today, as usual, he put

16

down his schoolbooks and started for the back of the house, where the laboratory was. But his mother's voice stopped him before he could get very far.

"Is that you, Danny?"

"Yes, Mom."

Mrs. Dunn came into the hall, wiping her hands on her apron. Her hair was as red as Danny's, and there were spots of flour on her cheeks.

"I've been making something special for to-night," she explained, giving her son a hug. "How'd things go today in school?"

"All right. What are you cooking, Mom?"

"Never mind." She held him off at arm's length. "Look at me," she commanded.

Danny did so, trying to grin.

"Daniel Dunn," said his mother. "Whenever I get that sickly smile from you, I know you've been up to something. More experiments?"

"No, Mom, honest."

"Nothing at all? Honest and truly?"

"We-e-ell." He blushed.

"Go on. What happened?" Mrs. Dunn demanded severely.

"Well, I was—I have to write a hundred sentences."

"Hmph! I can guess. 'I will not fight with people in the hallways.' Is that it?"

"No. I have to write, 'I will not daydream about space flight in class,' " said Danny. Then he added quickly, "But I can do it later, Mom. Where's Professor Bullfinch?"

"Hut-tut-tut!" cried Mrs. Dunn. "Don't let me hear you talk about the Professor. Not when you've your own work to do. March right into the kitchen where I can keep you under my eye until you get those sentences done. You're in the Professor's way quite enough as it is."

Danny marched. He sat down at the kitchen table and began slowly, with much labor, to write the first sentence.

"It smells too good in here to write all this stuff," he complained.

"Pineapple upside-down cake," said Mrs. Dunn. "The Professor is expecting some gentlemen to dinner. Just you go on writing." She folded her arms and frowned at Danny. "I'm ashamed of you. How do you ever expect to become a scientist like Professor Bullfinch if you won't pay attention in class? The last time I talked to Miss Arnold she said, 'Mrs. Dunn, I don't know what to do about Danny. He's very bright,' she said, 'but he's getting ahead of himself—trying to fly before he can walk.' Now I know what she meant. *Space* flying."

"But Mom," Danny said earnestly, "I can't help it. I want to find out how things work. She's just mad because I'm always experimenting or thinking about new things."

"You can't do new experiments until you know what others have done before you," Mrs. Dunn said. "Otherwise you might find yourself inventing the electric light all over again. If you want to go to college, you must first go to grammar school and high school."

She looked seriously at him. "Oh, Danny, Danny," she said, "it's hard enough for us. I'll back you up, I'll get you to college somehow, but it's going to be a struggle. You'll have to do your part by getting good marks. You do see that, don't you?"

Danny swallowed hard. "Yes, Mom," he replied. "I'll do my best from now on. I promise."

"All right." Mrs. Dunn briskly wiped the corners of her eyes with her apron. "Now, then. You'll never finish those sentences if you write them that way. Why don't you use the vertical method? That's what I used to do when I had to write sentences for school."

Danny blinked, trying to imagine Miss Arnold scolding his mother and making her write something a hundred times.

"What's the vertical method?" he asked.

"Why, first you write the first word a hundred times, one underneath another. Then the second word after it. Then the third, and so on. It's a lot easier to write 'I' a hundred times, and then go on to 'will,' than it is to write the whole thing out."

"Gee, Mom," Danny said in admiration, "you're a genius!"

"Go on, now," said Mrs. Dunn, grinning. "And you may as well finish up this leftover pineapple."

Danny had just written "daydream" for the fiftieth time when Professor Bullfinch came into the kitchen. Most people think of scientists as dreamy, long-haired, bearded, or otherwise curiously different from other men. Professor Bullfinch was bald, pink-faced, and tubby, with a jolly manner. He wore a tweed jacket and black-rimmed glasses, and he looked hungry.

"Smells awfully good in here," he said. "May I lick the bowl?"

"Sorry," said Mrs. Dunn. "There isn't any bowl to lick. And Danny has already eaten the leftovers. Now take your fingers out of my cake, Professor Bullfinch. You're worse than Danny."

Professor Bullfinch quickly pulled his hand out of the cake dish. "Remind me to work out a way of making my hands invisible," he said. "By the way, speaking of Danny—can you spare him for a few minutes? I have something to show him."

"I can spare him," said Mrs. Dunn, popping the cake into the oven, "but his schoolwork can't. He's got some sentences to finish."

"Grammar?"

"No. He has to write, 'I will not daydream about space flight in class' one hundred times."

"He daydreamed one hundred times about the same thing?" asked the Professor.

"No, no. I mean he has to write that out a hundred times."

"I see. Ridiculous! Why doesn't the school let the pupils use a mimeograph machine? It would be so much quicker than writing it out longhand."

"It's a punishment, Professor Bullfinch," Mrs. Dunn said patiently.

Professor Bullfinch tapped his chin thoughtfully. "A punishment for daydreaming about space flight? Good heavens! What will they

21

think of next? Why, that's all some of my colleagues do. It was because physicists daydreamed about space flight that we have the satellite up above us now.

"Great guns!" He clapped his hand to his head. "I completely forgot. The satellite! Of course! Come along, Danny."

He seized Danny's hand and pulled him bodily from his chair and through the door. Mrs. Dunn called, "Wait, Professor! His sentences!" But it was too late. They had both vanished. Mrs. Dunn sighed and shook her head, and then with a smile she put the unfinished paper up on a shelf.

CHAPTER THREE

The Rise of Professor Bullfinch

Professor Bullfinch's laboratory held many different kinds of instruments, for he was interested in all types of scientific knowledge. In one corner stood a large three-inch reflecting telescope on a tripod, which on starry nights he carried up to the roof. Now he had it pointing through a tall window.

He looked at his watch and adjusted the telescope. "Look," he said. "You can see it clearly."

"See what?" Danny asked.

"The satellite, of course. Didn't I tell you? It's in the sky now. Hurry. It won't be in view long."

Danny bent over and peered through the eyepiece. He saw a shining, silvery disk. As he watched, it moved across the lens and out of his field of vision.

"It looks like a moon," Danny said.

"It *is* a moon," said the Professor. "A manmade moon. Science has dreamed and worked for this moment."

Danny turned away from the telescope. "I wish I could be in it," he said. "To see what the earth looks like from up there."

Professor Bullfinch smiled at him. "It wouldn't be very comfortable," he remarked. "The satellite only measures about thirty inches in diameter. Besides, we'll have photographs of everything it sees."

"That's not the same thing. I want to see for myself."

"A very good idea." The Professor chuckled. "You've always been that way, Dan. I remember when you were about two years old, and your mother told you not to touch the stove because it was hot. You wanted to find out for yourself. You burned your finger, as I recall."

Danny laughed too. He said, "Yes, but you've told me yourself, lots of times, that a scientist is a man who's always trying to find things out for himself."

Professor Bullfinch nodded. He clasped his hands behind his back and began to walk up and down the room.

"Quite true," he said. "Sometimes knowledge is worth a burned finger. A scientist must always be asking, 'How? What? Why?' As a matter of fact, I've been asking myself those questions all day—especially 'Why?' "

"Why what?"

The Professor pointed to the stone-topped laboratory bench. On it, amongst a litter of equipment, was a metal stand on which was a glass beaker. It contained a curious liquid that glowed and quivered as if it were full of sunlight.

Danny walked over to stare at it.

"As you know," said the Professor, "I've been working on a type of insulating paint for rockets. I was positive I had it, and in fact I invited a Mr. Willoughby from the National Research Council to come and discuss it with me. But then, unexpectedly, this odd effect began this morning."

"What is it?" Danny said.

"I don't know. I've been waiting to see if it will do anything else."

The Professor paused with his head on one side, looking at the liquid. "I think I can understand why it glows," he said. "But why does it quiver?"

Danny leaned forward. "Listen, Professor," he said eagerly, reaching out toward the flask. "Maybe it's—"

"Look out!" cried Professor Bullfinch. "You're too—"

Danny's finger jerked. The flask, unbalanced, fell off its stand and crashed to the floor.

"—headstrong," Professor Bullfinch finished in a mild voice.

Danny stared in horror at what he had done. Splinters of glass were mixed with glowing globules of the liquid. Some of the quivering stuff dripped from the edge of the stone bench and formed a pool on the floor.

In all the years since he had first known the Professor, he had never seen him lose his temper. But, he reminded himself, there always has to be a first time for everything—and the first time is sometimes the worst. He was almost afraid to look up.

However, the Professor's face hadn't changed. It was as round and calm as ever. He said, "Accidents will happen, Dan. Here, give me a hand. Let's see if we can scoop up enough of it for analysis."

He was moving even as he spoke. Quickly he slipped on a pair of heavy gloves. He caught up a handful of test tubes from the bench. The glowing liquid was somewhat heavier than water

—more like light oil—and, working speedily, he was able to get quite a bit of it into the tubes.

He directed Danny to place a rack handy. He set the test tubes in the rack. Danny fetched a mop and cleaned up what was left on the floor. The Professor stuffed the mophead into the incinerator.

Then he turned to Danny. In a kindly voice he said, "Let's forget it, Dan. I was even worse at your age. They used to call me 'Bullhead Bullfinch,' and I got over it. There's not too much damage done. I may have to pick a little dust and fluff out of the stuff—that's all."

"I'm sorry," Danny said in a small voice.

"Don't worry about it." The Professor rumpled Danny's hair. "But you can file this away for the future: a scientist must spend a lot of time thinking and studying before he acts."

Danny nodded. "I understand. I won't do it again."

The Professor sighed. "I'll be satisfied if you don't do it again *today*," he said.

Before they could discuss the matter further, Mrs. Dunn poked her head in at the door.

"Company's here, Mr. Bullfinch," she said.

They all went down the hallway that led from the lab to the front of the house. In the living

27

room two men were waiting for the Professor. One was a tall, heavy-set, angry-looking man in a dark suit. The other seemed more pleasant and wore gold-rimmed spectacles, behind which his blue eyes sparkled cheerily.

The blue-eyed man said, "How do you do, Professor Bullfinch. I am Mr. Willoughby of the National Research Council. We spoke together on the phone."

"Ah, yes," said the Professor.

"And this," said Mr. Willoughby, indicating the angry-looking man, "is Dr. Grimes, President of the International Rocket Society."

"Of course," said the Professor. "Your name is certainly well known to me, Dr. Grimes."

"Thank you," growled Grimes.

The Professor stepped forward to shake hands. As his fingers touched those of Mr. Willoughby, there was a faint crackle. Mr. Willoughby snatched his hand away with a startled exclamation.

"Oh!" said Professor Bullfinch. "I'm—"

He had no time to say more. Before their astounded eyes he shot up off the floor. There was a dull thud as his head banged against the ceiling.

CHAPTER FOUR

"We Have Conquered Gravity!"

For a moment there was a stunned silence. Mr. Willoughby's mouth hung open like a new-caught fish's. Mrs. Dunn, who had been on her way to the kitchen, sank back against the wall, staring. Danny's eyes bulged. Only Dr. Grimes kept his stern and rigid expression.

Then Mr. Willoughby said weakly, "Er—Professor Bullfinch. What are you standing on?"

The Professor bent his head to look down at the others. He winced, for he had given himself a severe bump.

"It is difficult," he replied with irritation, "to say whether I am hanging, floating, or lying vertically. However, I am certainly not standing."

Dr. Grimes broke the silence. "It's a trick!" he said harshly. "Come down at once."

"Look here," said the Professor. "I don't see—"

"It is hardly dignified for a man in your position—" Dr. Grimes went on.

"Gentlemen, please!" Mr. Willoughby put in, as soothingly as he could. "Let's not argue." He stared up at the ceiling and said, with an effort to be calm, "Won't you try to come down, please, Professor?"

Professor Bullfinch raised his arms above his head and pushed against the ceiling. He pushed himself down to arm's length. The instant he stopped pushing, however, and dropped his arms, he bounced back up against the ceiling.

"Ow!" he yelled. "Drat it!"

Mrs. Dunn, who had been standing frozen in the corner, burst into hysterical laughter. She sank into a chair and threw her apron over her head. Mr. Willoughby wrung his hands, but Dr. Grimes, with a sour look, stepped to her side. He shook her by the shoulder.

"Madam, control yourself!" he barked.

Mrs. Dunn took the apron down from her face and gasped, "I'm sorry. After all these years I ought to be used to anything. But he looks so— so *helpless* up there."

"Well," Dr. Grimes said grimly, "I'll soon get him down. He can't fool me with his gymnastics."

He reached up and caught hold of the Professor's ankles. Red-faced and puffing from the effort, he pulled him down a few feet.

He reached up and caught hold of the Professor's
ankles

"There!" he said.

He let go of the Professor's legs.

Mr. Willoughby shouted, "There he goes again!"

Professor Bullfinch soared upwards. This time he was able to protect his head with his arms.

"For heaven's sake!" he cried. "That's enough!"

"Ropes," said Dr. Grimes, looking furiously up at him. "Ropes and counterweights. That's how he does it."

"What do you think the ropes are attached to?" said the Professor.

Grimes began to splutter. "They don't have to be attached to anything. It's mass hypnosis, like the Indian rope trick. I refuse to be hypnotized. I refuse, do you hear?"

The Professor could not help smiling. "I'm still here, Dr. Grimes," he said.

Danny had been too startled and fascinated to talk. Now he burst out, "But Professor! You can't just hang there!"

"I'm not too uncomfortable," the Professor replied. "Do you suppose you could get me my pipe? It's over in the laboratory, on the bench."

Danny ran to get it.

Dr. Grimes, who had been listening with a

scowl, said, "Aha! The pipe must be part of the trick."

Mrs. Dunn had regained control of herself. She looked up at the Professor, clasping her hands together, and said, "Oh, dear, can't we *do* something?"

The Professor said, "Don't be upset, Mrs. Dunn. While I'm up here, I'll change the bulbs in the chandelier. I promised you I'd do it yesterday, but I forgot."

"How can you joke, Professor Bullfinch?" she cried.

"Why not?" said the Professor. "It isn't really that serious."

Nevertheless, he began to look a little worried.

Danny came panting back with the pipe. He climbed on a chair and handed it to the Professor. He did not get down again, however. Instead, he said, "Professor Bullfinch. You know what?"

"Yes," said the Professor. "I'm beginning to get a stiff neck from trying to look down."

"But listen, Professor—"

"Please, Danny. Remember your promise."

"But—"

"I must think. This is absurd. Why am I up here? Let me try to think out exactly what happened."

"But—"

The Professor stuck his unlighted pipe in his mouth. He pressed his hands to his temples. "I entered the room," he muttered to himself. "Walked over to Willoughby. Shook hands. There was a spark of static electricity, probably caused by the rubbing of my shoes on the carpet."

"Listen—" said Danny.

The Professor was deep in thought and did not hear him. "Rubbing feet on carpet—electric shock—is it possible that that small shock could have caused me to rise? Why? Or could it have had something to do with my shoes?"

At this point Danny shouted, "That's what I've been trying to tell you! The soles of your shoes—"

"What?"

"They're glowing and quivering! Just like the stuff in that flask! You must have stepped in it when we were cleaning it up!"

"What are you talking about?" said Dr. Grimes.

Mr. Willoughby said, "What do you mean?"

"I mean," Danny said, in a businesslike way, "that now we can get the Professor down."

Still on the chair, he reached up and unlaced the Professor's shoes.

"Wait a minute!" cried Professor Bullfinch, as Danny slipped both his shoes off. "Remember what I said! I think—"

The shoes flew out of Danny's hands and stuck to the ceiling.

"—we have conquered gravity!" the Professor shouted, and crashed to the floor.

CHAPTER FIVE

Top Secret

Groaning a little, Professor Bullfinch got to his feet. He rubbed his back and cautiously bent his arms and legs.

"Danny," he said in a dry voice.

Danny's face was red. "I—I was excited," he stuttered. "Gosh, who wouldn't be?"

Mr. Willoughby was shaking his head in a bewildered manner. "I still don't understand it," he said.

Mrs. Dunn had jumped to her feet when the Professor fell to the floor. She came over to him now and asked anxiously, "Are you all right?"

"Certainly. Just a bit shaken up—or down, as the case may be."

He smiled, and began looking for his pipe.

Mr. Willoughby said, "Professor Bullfinch, for goodness sake, please tell me what this is all about. I can hardly believe, even now, what I saw."

He looked up. The Professor's shoes were still clinging to the ceiling. The strange, glowing liquid could be plainly seen on their soles.

Dr. Grimes snapped his fingers. "I've got it!" he cried. "Static electricity! You gave it away yourself."

"Yes," said the Professor seriously, "I believe you're right. When I rubbed my feet on the carpet, I built up a charge of static electricity in my body. In some way this was enough to charge that liquid on my shoes."

Dr. Grimes sneered, "Rubbish! Have you got a deck of cards?"

"Why—I believe so," said Mrs. Dunn. "But—"

Dr. Grimes rubbed his hands together. "Give them to me at once, please."

Mrs. Dunn glanced at Professor Bullfinch, and he nodded. She opened the drawer of the sideboard and got out a deck of playing cards.

Dr. Grimes snatched them. He took out one and, holding it, rubbed his feet on the carpet.

"This is hardly the time," Mr. Willoughby protested, "for card tricks. Really, Dr. Grimes, I think—"

The grim-faced rocket expert was not listening. After he had rubbed his feet for a while on the carpet, he placed the card against the smooth surface of the living-room wall. It clung to the wall for a moment or two before fluttering to the floor.

"There you are!" Dr. Grimes said triumphantly. "Static electricity has made the card stick to the wall. The same thing is true for the shoes."

Professor Bullfinch chuckled. Then, standing on the chair, he reached up. He took hold of one of the shoes and, with an obvious effort, forced it away from the ceiling. He carried it to a window. He looked very odd indeed, for the hand in which he held the shoe stuck straight up above his head, and he himself barely touched the floor as he walked.

"Danny," he called. "Open this window, please."

Danny hurried to do as he was asked.

"Now then, the rest of you," said the Professor. "Quickly, for I can't hold this shoe much longer. Mr. Willoughby, Dr. Grimes—you open the other window and watch."

"Watch what?" said Mr. Willoughby.

Dr. Grimes flung the window open and thrust his head outside. Mr. Willoughby and Mrs. Dunn crowded next to him. Danny, crouching at the sill of the first window, ducked his head so that the Professor could lean out.

The shoe rose swiftly in the evening air

Professor Bullfinch held the shoe out the window and opened his hand. It was as if he had released a balloon. The shoe rose swiftly in the evening air, catching the last rays of the sun on its surface, and then vanished from their sight.

For once Dr. Grimes had nothing to say. But Mr. Willoughby, in excitement, slammed down the window—almost catching Dr. Grimes's head in it—and cried, "Spectacular! Amazing! My dear Professor, this is unbelievable!"

"It is, isn't it?" said the Professor calmly.

"How did you do it?"

"I'm not quite sure. This liquid appears to have strange properties." The Professor began pacing up and down. "I'll have to do a number of experiments tomorrow in an attempt to find out just how it works." He stopped and faced the others. "But it seems clear to me that, among other things, we may have the solution to the problem of space flight."

Danny's eyes widened. "S-space flight!" he shouted.

The Professor raised his hand. "I said *may*," he cautioned. "I have no idea yet whether it will be practical. We don't know how long the effect lasts. That shoe may come tumbling down on our heads by tomorrow morning. We'll leave it on the ceiling, for the time being, for observation. I have no notion of what the force of the liquid is, or whether it must be continuously charged with electricity, or—or about anything," he finished rather helplessly. He threw out his arms. "All I know is that it appears to cut off the power of gravity."

Mr. Willoughby drew a long breath. "Space flight," he repeated. "By George, it's—it's *big*. Too big to swallow all at once. One thing I do know, though: I'll have to notify Washington."

He glanced at his watch. "Too late now. I'm afraid there'll be no one in the office. First thing tomorrow morning, then. Meanwhile, there's one thing I must stress."

He looked round at them, his eyes sober behind the gold-rimmed spectacles. "I must ask you all—especially you, young man"—nodding at Danny—"to be very circumspect about this—this effect."

"I promise," Danny said promptly. "What does 'circumspect' mean? To look it over carefully?"

"That's 'inspect,'" said the Professor. "No, Mr. Willoughby means we mustn't say anything to anyone about it. It will have to remain a secret for the time being. You mustn't breathe a word of it, not even to your best friend—what's his name?—that boy who always looks so sad."

"Joe Pearson. Not even to Joe?"

"No. Will you promise? On your honor as a —as a scientist, Dan?"

Danny nodded solemnly.

"Well, then, that's settled," said Willoughby. "I'll put through a long-distance call tomorrow. We will have to get a research grant." He took off his glasses and wiped them carefully. "If there is a possibility of space flight, we'll need money for the construction of a ship. A ship to the stars!" He looked up at the shoe on the ceiling. "Great heavens," he said. "The excitement has worn me out. I feel quite exhausted."

"Well, no wonder," said Mrs. Dunn in a practical tone. "It's long past dinner time. I think we'd all be the better for a mouthful of food."

"Well spoken," said the Professor. "Do I remember something about pineapple upside-down cake? Dr. Grimes, Mr. Willoughby, after you gentlemen." He motioned to the dining room.

Dr. Grimes snorted. "Do you propose to begin experiments on this—this so-called anti-gravity effect, tonight?"

"Tomorrow morning will be time enough," said the Professor.

"Then I must ask you to put me up," Dr. Grimes said bluntly. "I have no intention of leaving you to rig up any tricks behind my back."

The Professor frowned. Then he controlled his annoyance and said quietly, "Dr. Grimes, you have spent so much time in rocket research that I can understand your feelings about this new material. You are welcome to stay here as long as you like and to work with me on all experiments. It will be valuable, no doubt, for me to have someone to check all my work. Does that satisfy you?"

Dr. Grimes could never apologize. But he grunted, "Thank you. Most generous." Which was as close as he could come to admitting he might have acted rudely.

It was nearly eleven o'clock when Danny at last went up to bed. Downstairs he could hear the three men still talking and arguing loudly. They were planning a series of experiments for the morning. He undressed and brushed his teeth. Before he got into bed he opened the window and looked out. Above him the sky was brilliant with stars. Somewhere among those glowing, twinkling points of light one of Professor Bull-finch's shoes sailed, on and out, away from the familiar earth.

"A ship to the stars," Danny murmured to himself.

Then, with a chuckle, he jumped into bed and, before his imagination could begin to work, he was asleep.

CHAPTER SIX

An Odd Duet

The next day began badly for Danny.

In the first place, he was so excited by the events of the night before that, once he got his eyes properly open, he didn't want to go to school, knowing what would be happening at home. It was with difficulty that Mrs. Dunn bundled him out of the house. When he got to school, he was ten minutes late.

Then, as if that weren't enough, he discovered that he had forgotten his hundred sentences. He couldn't even remember where he had left them. Miss Arnold did her best to be patient, but in the end she said, "I'm sorry, Dan, but you'll have to learn to take assignments like that more seriously. Tomorrow—no, tomorrow is Saturday—very well, Monday, I want to see those sentences and another fifty saying, 'I must remember to bring in my work.' "

When he started for home at three o'clock, Danny felt as if all the sorrows of the world rested on his shoulders. Joe Pearson's first words did nothing to make him feel better.

"Gosh," Joe muttered, as they walked up a tree-shaded alley together, "that Miss Arnold— where some people have a sense of humor, she's got a sense of gravity."

"Gravity?" Danny said with a start. The word reminded him at once of the Professor's discovery.

"You know what I mean, she always takes everything so seriously."

"Oh, sure, sure." Danny bit his lip, remembering his solemn promise to keep silence.

Joe moodily kicked at a stone. "Of course, it's your fault too, Danny. You always have your feet off the ground."

"Huh?"

Joe nodded. "Take it easy. Remember, what goes up must come down."

"Urp!" said Danny.

"Look at that, now. A hundred and fifty sentences! And on a weekend too."

"Listen, Joe," Danny began. "I—listen, suppose—"

"Suppose what?"

Danny gulped. He had given his word, after all, on his honor as a scientist.

"Nothing," he said.

Joe looked sideways at him. "Boy, you're really dizzy. See that? Nothing but trouble. It all started with that spaceship stuff yesterday—"

"Eep!" Danny couldn't help himself. Then he clamped his lips shut. Luckily Joe wasn't paying attention.

"—and this is where you wind up. What's the matter? Did you get into trouble last night when you got home?"

"Trouble? Oh—I—why—" The effort of trying not to talk about the anti-gravity fluid, when every word brought it to mind, made great beads of sweat stand out on Danny's forehead.

"Hey, I gotta run," he blurted at last. "My mother promised to bake me if I didn't get home."

"What?"

"I mean, she's going to lick a cake. I mean—anyway, I've just *got* to go. I have to do about a thillion mings—I mean a million thills—"

He wiped his face. "So long, Joe. See you tomorrow, maybe," he gasped.

Then he ran for home, leaving Joe staring, openmouthed, after him. But for once Danny couldn't spare the time to worry about what his friend thought; he was too busy wondering what was going on in the laboratory.

The lab, when he poked his head cautiously in at the door, was a peculiar sight.

Almost half of the equipment was stuck to the ceiling. To some of the pieces long wires leading to rows of batteries on the tables were attached, so that the place looked as if it were decorated with balloons and streamers for a party. The floor was littered with broken glass. A long ladder stood in the center of the room. Professor Bullfinch and Dr. Grimes sat in the middle of the room in their shirt sleeves, with their neckties hanging loose. They looked exhausted.

The Professor was saying, "We have tried every possible experiment. You must admit that the liquid cuts off gravity."

Dr. Grimes was hoarse. "I will admit only that it *appears* to do so," he said stubbornly. "Nothing else has been proved. The whole effect may be caused by—by sunspots, for instance."

"Come, come, Grimes," said the Professor patiently. "We have found that, unless the electrical charge is constantly renewed in an object, the effect is temporary—"

"Ha!" Grimes said. "And we do not yet know that it can ever be permanent."

At that moment a glass flask which was clinging to a corner of the ceiling suddenly fell to the floor with a crash. The two scientists paid no attention to it but went on arguing as if nothing had happened.

"Time will tell," said the Professor. "If we keep a small charge passing through some of these objects and observe them constantly during the next few weeks—"

He broke off, seeing Danny for the first time.

"I think it's time we took a rest," he said. "Hello, Dan. As you came in, did you happen to notice whether my shoe is still on the living-room ceiling?"

"Yes, it is, Professor."

The Professor rose to his feet. "Come, Dr. Grimes," he said, "let's declare a truce. I know I'm tired, and you have climbed up and down that ladder so often this afternoon that you must be quite worn out."

"Not at all," said Grimes. "I feel very fresh."

But when he stood up, he was so tired that he staggered and had to steady himself on the back of the chair.

They went into the living room. As they entered, the Professor's shoe dropped from the ceiling. It landed at his feet with a thump. He picked it up.

Danny said, "Professor! Maybe your other shoe will come falling back into the front yard!"

"I'm afraid not," Professor Bullfinch replied. "If it has not flown completely outside the zone of earth's gravity and should come falling back, it would probably be burned up as it passed through the earth's atmosphere, just as a meteorite is." He shook his head. "Some people give their bodies to science. I have given a shoe. They were good shoes too."

Mrs. Dunn brought in some tea and toast, and some milk and cookies for Danny.

"Mom, have you seen those sentences I wrote yesterday for school?" Danny asked.

"Oh, oh!" his mother said. "I forgot and tucked them up on a shelf in the kitchen. Did you get into hot water over them?"

Danny nodded. "I'm supposed to write fifty more saying, 'I must remember to bring in my work.'"

"Oh, dear." Mrs. Dunn patted her son's shoulder. "We were so confused and excited last night that it's a wonder we didn't all forget our heads. I'll phone Miss Arnold and explain that it was my fault. Perhaps she'll let you off."

Professor Bullfinch was saying earnestly to Dr. Grimes, "How do you feel about music?"

"Why do you ask?"

"Well, my favorite relaxation is the bull fiddle. I was wondering if you'd mind if I played some music."

For the first time since his arrival Dr. Grimes's face softened. The angry look disappeared, his eyebrows rose, and slowly, as if it hurt him to do so, he smiled.

"Well!" he said. "As it happens, I am very fond of music."

"Good," said the Professor. "I'll get my fiddle."

"I hope," Dr. Grimes said, "that you will allow me to play along with you."

"On the fiddle? I'm afraid there isn't room," said Professor Bullfinch. "Only one at a time—"

"No, no. I didn't mean that." Dr. Grimes reached into the inside pocket of his jacket and brought out a small leather case. "I play the piccolo for relaxation, as it happens."

"Splendid!" cried the Professor.

He went to a closet and brought out his bull fiddle. He tuned it and played a few notes. Meantime Dr. Grimes had fitted together his piccolo, and now he blew a few runs on it. They looked very odd together: Dr. Grimes, tall and portly and red-faced, with the tiny piccolo at his lips, and Professor Bullfinch, round and fat, straining up to reach the neck of the bull fiddle, which was much taller than he was.

Then they began to play. They started with a lively dance, the piccolo squealing shrilly, the bull fiddle zoom-zooming darkly. The combination reminded Danny of a small and active kitten racing round a big Saint Bernard.

When they had finished, they mopped their foreheads and began a slower piece. Then they played a quick melody. Louder and faster they played, tapping their feet and nodding their heads. Suddenly they were interrupted by a loud crash.

"What was that?" asked the Professor.

Mrs. Dunn, who had been listening with a smile from the doorway, hastened into the room.

"Your lovely glass vase!" she clucked sympathetically. "How on earth did it happen? It was standing on the edge of the sideboard."

She began to collect the pieces of broken glass.

"I wonder," said the Professor, "if possibly a high note from the piccolo broke the glass."

"How could it do that?" Danny asked.

"Well, the vibration of a high note can cause glass to vibrate in sympathy."

"Nonsense!" Dr. Grimes began to bristle.

"It is much more likely that the vibrations from a low note on the bull fiddle caused the sideboard to vibrate, and shook the vase off."

"My dear Grimes," said the Professor, "it's a matter of pitch. And a shrill note *can* shatter glass."

Dr. Grimes glared. "Are you suggesting that my piccolo is shrill?"

"It is certainly not low-toned," said the Professor mildly. "But the bull fiddle—"

"The bull fiddle is only fit for accompaniment," said Dr. Grimes. "The pitch is so low—"

"Yes, but the pitch of the piccolo is so high—" the Professor interrupted.

Luckily, at that instant the doorbell rang. The two scientists stopped their quarrel, while Mrs. Dunn went to the door. They heard Mr. Willoughby's voice greeting her, and next moment he came into the room.

"Good afternoon!" he cried, beaming at them. "A happy little concert party, eh? I am delighted to see that you two gentlemen have become so friendly. No more arguments, eh? Good, good!"

Dr. Grimes began to put his piccolo away. "Well, what's the news, Willoughby?" he said.

"I won't keep you in suspense. The news is

good. Washington has decided to give priority to experiments with the—er—the anti-gravity fluid. And if—mind you, I say *if*—it appears that we have something suitable for space travel, then funds will be provided for the construction of a spaceship."

"Excellent!" Professor Bullfinch looked very pleased.

"I am to be in charge of the project," Mr. Willoughby continued. "That is, I will have to make regular reports on progress. Dr. Grimes, we shall retain you as advisor. And now, Professor Bullfinch, the rest is up to you."

And solemnly, although his blue eyes were sparkling behind his glasses, he held out his hand.

Professor Bullfinch shook it. "This time," he remarked, "I hope we can finish our handshake without my bumping against the ceiling."

Mr. Willoughby looked round at the rest.

"One more point," he said, and suddenly his expression became very grave. "I have mentioned this before, but now we are official. There is one word you must live with from now on: secrecy. Secrecy is our watchword, night and day!"

CHAPTER SEVEN

It's Tomorrow

Secrecy is our watchword. The words rang in Danny's ears, and for the next three months or so he was both more happy and more miserable than any other boy in the land. Happy, because he was on the inside of one of the most thrilling projects ever begun by man, and miserable, because he had to keep a constant watch over himself to be sure he never let anything slip out about it.

Professor Bullfinch, with his constant companion, Dr. Grimes, spent more and more time in the laboratory testing and analyzing the anti-gravity liquid. It became clear that whatever was painted with the liquid resisted gravity and would fly out away from the earth. As long as the paint was charged with electricity, the liquid continued to operate. The speed of the object could be controlled by regulating the strength of the electrical charge in it.

Dr. Grimes and the Professor argued for hours over how an anti-gravity ship would look and what it would carry. At last the day came when Danny, sitting on a stool with his elbows on the lab bench and his chin on his hands, was allowed to look at the large charts and drawings they had prepared.

"You see," the Professor explained, "this ship will not look like most people's idea of a spaceship. In the first place, we won't have to worry about either friction or acceleration."

"I don't understand, Professor," Danny said.

"Well, a rocket ship needs to get away from the pull of gravity, and so it must go very fast until it's free. But the heat caused by the friction of the atmosphere might burn it up. That's the first problem. Second, that great starting speed means that the men in the ship will have to undergo tremendous pressure.

"We, however, can go just as fast or as slowly as we like, since the anti-gravity paint overcomes the earth's pull. Our ship will have an automatic governor, so that when we start it it will automatically travel very slowly, and then gradually gather speed as it goes higher. There will be almost no sense of movement, no pressure, and we can go slowly enough so that air friction will be no danger."

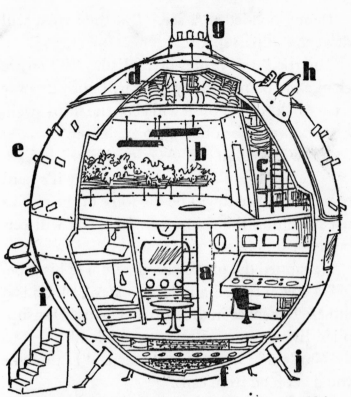

Diagram of First Anti-Gravity Space Ship

a Main living quarters—galley, bunks,
   control panel, ports, etc.
b Hydroponic garden
c Storeroom
d Machinery for heating, air circulation, etc.
e Belt of rocket exhausts
f Weighted base containing fuel tanks
   pumps, interior electrical system
g Solar battery & antennae
h TV system on mobile tracks
i Hatch entry
j Telescopic legs

Danny nodded. "I see. But then what will drive the ship in space?"

"Inertia," the Professor replied. "When we charge the paint, gravity itself will push us away from earth. That push will keep the ship—well, *coasting* would be one way to explain it."

"How fast will it go? As fast as light?"

"Oh, no, I don't think so. Actually it's hard to say, but since it will be the force of the earth's mass pushing the ship away, its speed will certainly be immense."

He tapped the plans with the stem of his pipe.

"We won't need any fuel to speak of, and so most of our space in the ship will be used for supplies, living quarters, and our garden."

"Garden?" Danny exclaimed. "I thought you'd get food from cans."

"So we will, to a certain extent." The Professor smiled. "But fresh food and flowers are important to men cooped up in a limited amount of space like this. Anyway, that's what I think. And this garden will also act as an important extra air supply."

"How can it do that?"

"Well, plants under light, when they are making food for themselves, release a great deal of oxygen. Now, we'll make most of our oxygen from chemicals, but the garden will produce a certain amount of fresh air and will absorb a certain amount of the carbon dioxide breathed out by the passengers."

Danny grinned. "Then most of your space will be taken up by a load of dirt."

"No, no. The plants will grow in water to which certain chemicals have been added that will give the plants all they need to feed on."

"Gosh," Danny murmured. "I never thought a spaceship would be a flying back yard. And what's that thing sticking out of the top of the hull?"

"That's a solar battery. Since we only need a small amount of current for charging the anti-gravity paint, we are going to draw it from the sun. That way we'll never run out of electricity, and there'll be no danger of our suddenly falling back to earth, or onto the Moon."

"The Moon?"

"Yes, Danny. After a couple of test flights, the first trip will be to the Moon and back—non-stop."

Danny drew a deep breath. Then the question which had been simmering inside him for a long time popped out: "I—I don't suppose," he said, "you'd want to take a—a boy along on your trip?"

The Professor had been lighting his pipe. He began to cough and choke. When he could catch his breath, he said, "Danny, my boy! You don't think *I'm* going on that first flight, do you?"

"Aren't you?"

"No indeed. I'm a physicist, not a test pilot. I wouldn't have the slightest idea what to do in an emergency." He shook his head. "I must say, I wouldn't mind going. But the government has decided that the first flight will be piloted by a man who is an expert in the field. He's a rocket pilot named Joseph Beach, a lieutenant colonel in the Air Force."

"Oh," Danny said in a subdued voice. "And I guess he wouldn't want a copilot, huh?"

"He'll have a copilot. A major named Albert Baum."

Danny shook his head sadly.

The Professor put an arm around his shoulders. "Some day, my boy," he said. "Just be patient."

"All right," said Danny, making the best of it. "Anyway, I should at least get through junior high school first."

It began to look as if Danny would not only get through junior high but be an honor student as well. To keep his mind off his problems, he concentrated on schoolwork with more energy than ever before. And one day in class even Miss Arnold commented on it.

"You certainly have come a long way in the last few months, Danny," she said. "You have been very steady and attentive, and this last theme you wrote on 'My Favorite Pet' was one of the best in the class. Only, I have one question to ask. Do you *really* have a pet firefly?"

There was no reply. Miss Arnold looked more closely at Danny. His eyes were fixed on the blackboard, and they were glazed as if he were in a trance.

"Daniel Dunn!" Miss Arnold said sharply.

Danny jumped. "Huh? What?" he gasped.

Miss Arnold frowned. "Danny," she said, "I'm afraid you weren't listening to me."

Danny gulped. With a sinking heart he said, "No, ma'am."

"You were daydreaming again, weren't you?"

"Yes, ma'am."

"About space flight?"

Silently he nodded. He had the best excuse in the world, but he couldn't give it, for in truth secrecy had been his watchword. Keeping the secret was his first thought each morning and his last at night.

Miss Arnold was looking angry. "Really, Danny, you don't leave me any alternative but to punish you. I was just telling you how much better you have been behaving, and you didn't even hear me because you were back in outer space. This time I think we'll have to make it three hundred sentences. You will please write, 'Space flight is a hundred years away.'"

"Hey!" All the secrecy Danny had bottled up exploded out of him at these words. "But it isn't. It's *tomorrow!*"

Miss Arnold's eyebrows slowly rose. "What?" she said.

Danny felt like biting off his tongue.

"What did you say?" Miss Arnold asked.

"Nothing," he said sullenly.

"I'm afraid we'd better make that five hundred sentences," said Miss Arnold. "I really don't think I can bring myself to believe that the first space flight will take place *tomorrow.*"

CHAPTER EIGHT

Joe Finds Out

When school was out, Joe Pearson tried to catch Danny at the classroom door, but he was too late. For the last two or three weeks Danny had been avoiding him, and Joe couldn't imagine why.

"Golly," Joe said to himself, "he's done it again. What's been eating him lately?"

He walked home slowly. He was wondering if he had done something to hurt Danny's feelings, or to make his friend angry with him.

Then he thought, "Well, there's only one way to find out. That's to ask him."

He stopped at home just long enough to eat a couple of doughnuts and get his bicycle. Then he set off for Danny's place. He rode his bike along the pleasant, tree-shaded streets until he came to the corner of Beckforth Road, on the edge of town, where the Professor's house stood. Past the house the road went fifteen miles through almost deserted countryside to Beckforth, a little village among the hills.

Joe was just about to cross to the Professor's

house when he saw a flash of light a little way up the road. Shading his eyes, he peered that way. The flash was a reflection from a bicycle he recognized at once. It was Danny, pedaling at full speed up the road toward Beckforth.

Joe could think of no reason in the world why his friend should go in that direction.

Then, suddenly, he thought, "Gosh! Maybe he's decided to run away from home!"

It was a dreadful idea. Something must be wrong, terribly wrong—something Joe couldn't even guess at. He gulped. Then he said to himself, "I can't let him go alone. I'll go with him."

He jumped on his bike again without a second thought and set off after Danny. But his friend had a long head start.

They rode on in this way, about half a mile apart, Danny never once looking back but hunched over his bike and going like the wind. Soon Joe was puffing. He bent to his work, and the perspiration streamed down his face. He had to slow down for a moment to wipe his eyes. When he had done so, he glanced ahead. Danny had disappeared.

He rode on, utterly bewildered. All at once he saw Danny's bike, lying in the grass by the side of the road.

Joe skidded to a halt. A thick woods came down to the very edge of the road, separated from it by a tumble-down stone wall. Leaving his bike beside Danny's, Joe climbed the wall and entered the woods. Some crushed and broken ferns told him his friend must have gone that way.

He walked a little distance, keeping a sharp eye out for footprints or other marks. The ground sloped up and the trees began to thin. Suddenly he emerged on the edge of a broad meadow. There were a few tall trees and a large red barn, its paint faded and a gaping space where its roof had been. But this wasn't what attracted Joe's attention.

He saw Danny running across the meadow toward the barn. Then he saw a man step out from behind a tree. Danny and the man talked for a moment and then went to the barn. The man knocked, and one of the large sliding doors opened. Professor Bullfinch stepped out. Joe saw him talking to Danny and then shaking his head. Danny turned and sadly walked back toward the woods.

But in the time between the opening and shutting of the door, Joe had seen something that made his hair stand on end.

It was a large metal globe, shining in the light that streamed through the open roof of the barn.

In a flash everything became clear—Danny's behavior in the past weeks, his strange answers to Joe, his speech in class that very afternoon.

"Holy leaping creepers!" Joe breathed. "Professor Bullfinch has invented a real, honest-to-goodness spaceship!"

CHAPTER NINE

Lost

Danny trudged back, kicking at loose stones. He stopped to glance at the barn. Then he almost jumped out of his skin, for a voice behind him said, "Hey, Dan!"

He whirled. "Joe!" he said. "Where—where'd you come from?"

Joe's eyes were dancing. "Gosh! Why didn't you tell me?" he cried.

"Tell you?" Danny said cautiously.

"About what's in the barn."

"What?"

"I followed you. I didn't mean to spy on you —I thought you were running away from home. But when the Professor opened the barn door, I saw it."

"Just what do you think you saw?" Danny asked.

"Aw, Dan, quit kidding around. I know a spaceship when I see one," said Joe.

"Oh." Danny rubbed his nose. Then he said, "You saw the ship? Gee, Joe, you're in trouble. It's a strict secret—a *government* secret."

All Joe's enthusiasm evaporated, and his face returned to its usual gloom. "Ooh. What do you think they'll do to me? Shoot me at dawn, maybe?"

"No. I don't think Professor Bullfinch would let them do *that*. Anyway, I don't think anybody saw you. And I won't say anything." He pulled Joe further into the shadows of the woods. "Now listen. First of all, I'm glad I didn't tell you anything about it. I've kept my mouth shut all this time, and now you'll have to swear to do the same."

Joe nodded.

"Raise your right hand," Danny ordered.

Joe did so.

"Do you, Joseph Pearson, solemnly swear by your right hand and blood to keep this deadly secret and never say a word to anybody, so help you?"

"I swear," Joe said in a voice that sounded as if it were coming from underground.

"O.K. But I sure hope nobody ever finds out. Honest, Joe, if you ever let anything slip, *I* may be shot at dawn."

They began walking back through the woods.

"Why didn't the Professor let you in?" Joe asked.

"Well, generally they let me hang around and watch them," Danny said. "But the first trial flight of the ship is going to be sometime in the next twenty-four hours, so they made me leave. Mr. Willoughby, the head of the project, said that strict secrecy requires it." As he said this, Danny imitated Willoughby's voice.

"He's never trusted me," he went on. "He said a couple of times he doesn't really think a kid can keep a secret as big as this. But the Professor told him I could. And I did, too."

"You sure did," Joe said. "I thought you were mad at me for some reason, or crazy, or something."

They came to the road and found their bicycles.

Danny said, "I've got to get home. I want to get those sentences out of the way tonight so I can be free tomorrow to watch the ship take off."

"Will they let you watch?"

"No, they don't want me around. But I know a way to get to the barn without the guards' seeing me. There are security guards from the government around the building, you know."

"Yes, I saw one of them talk to you."

69

"Well, I found an old culvert that runs right up under the barn, and I get in that way sometimes when I don't want Willoughby to know."

They pedaled along in silence for a few minutes, and then Joe said, "Listen. Suppose I come home with you and help you with the sentences?"

"Help me? How?"

"To write 'em. I can imitate your handwriting. Anyway, Miss Arnold won't know the difference. You know teachers never read those sentences."

"That doesn't matter. It wouldn't be honest," Dan said.

"The whole thing isn't honest," said Joe. "Space flight *is* tomorrow, like you told her in the first place."

"Hmm." Dan thought that over. Then he said, "Well, yes. That's true. Okay, let's hurry."

They whizzed along, and Danny shouted, "Rockets away! Ten, nine, eight—"

"Lay off, will you?" Joe panted. "Let's not play spaceship now—"

"—three, two, one, zero! Fire!" Danny yelled. "Whoops! My starboard rockets are missing."

He began to swerve his bike back and forth.

70

"Come on, Joe," he called. "You'd better bring your ship alongside. There are meteors crashing against my hull."

"I don't want to—" Joe began.

Just then Danny's bike hit a stone. His wheel wobbled and the bike skidded. Down he went by the side of the road.

"I knew it, I knew it, I knew it," Joe groaned, coming to a halt. "What did you break?"

Danny got up and dusted himself off. "Not a thing."

"Not even an arm?"

"Nope. Just bumped."

"Well, maybe your bike is smashed up, then," Joe said with dark satisfaction. "I told you—"

"Not a thing wrong with it," Danny said cheerfully.

He jumped on again. "Okay, no more rocket ships for now. Meteors are too thick here. Let's go."

They reached home with no further accidents, and Danny asked his mother if Joe could stay to dinner. Mrs. Dunn called Mrs. Pearson and arranged matters, and the two boys went up to Danny's room to work.

They kept at it furiously, doing twenty sentences to a page, using Mrs. Dunn's vertical

71

method. There were a few interruptions—dinner, for instance—but by eight o'clock they put down their pencils and looked wearily at each other over twenty-five pages of sentences.

"Boy!" Joe said. "I've got 'a hundred years' on the brain. I don't think I'll ever be able to listen to the words 'space flight' again."

Danny gathered up the pages. "Now I know how Professor Bullfinch feels after he works on formulas," he said. "It's a good thing we're both young and strong."

Joe rolled over on the bed. "I feel old and weak," he mumbled. "I don't think I'm long for this world."

Danny just laughed. "I've got an idea that'll revive you, Joe. How about coming over first thing tomorrow?"

He lowered his voice. "How would you like to see the first spaceship leave earth?"

"Oh, boy! Sure!" Joe said. "But how? You said they don't want you around."

"Yes. But you and I can watch from the edge of the woods. I'll try to find out when they plan the take-off. Nobody will know we're watching. What do you say?"

Joe sat up. "Great! Are you sure we can get away with it?"

"Oh, yes. You come as early as you can. Whistle like a robin for me under the window."

Joe got up to go. Danny added, "Remember Joe—secrecy is our watchword."

Joe nodded.

"And Joe—" Danny scratched his nose thoughtfully. "Thanks a million. I'd never have finished these sentences if it weren't for you."

"Ah, forget it," Joe said, grinning. "What's a friend for?"

Promptly the next morning, while the grass was still wet, Joe whistled secretly like a robin under Danny's window. Mrs. Dunn stuck her head out of the kitchen window and said, "Come on in, Joe. Danny's eating breakfast. I'm sure you can do with a pancake."

"No, thank you, Mrs. Dunn," Joe replied, wondering how she had guessed it was he. "I'm not hungry."

He forced himself to be polite, however, and ate six pancakes, with butter and syrup, and drank a glass of milk.

After breakfast the boys went into the living room. Danny asked softly, "All set?"

"Yes."

"Now you can imagine how I felt when Miss Arnold caught me in a daze yesterday."

"I know. You were thinking about today."

"Yep. And when she said I had to write, 'Space flight—' "

" '—is a hundred years away.' Don't ever say that sentence to me again."

"Thank goodness it's over and done with."

Danny turned to the bookcase. "Twenty-five pages! Look at the size of the paper clip I had to put on—"

His voice trailed off.

"What's the matter?" Joe asked.

Danny's face was pale.

"The sentences!" he gasped. "I *know* I brought them downstairs! I put them right there on top of the bookcase! And now they're gone!"

CHAPTER TEN

And Found

Joe turned green. "No," he said. "They can't be! All that work—"

"L-l-let's not g-g-get excited," Danny stammered. Then an idea struck him. "I'll look upstairs. Maybe I left them on the bed."

He dashed into the hall and pounded up the steps. In a few minutes he came thumping down again. "No. Not there."

He flew into the kitchen, with Joe at his heels.

"Mom!" he cried. "Have you seen my sentences?"

Mrs. Dunn paused in the midst of breaking an egg. "Oh, Danny, not *again*," she said. "This time it wasn't my fault, I'm sure. Where did you leave them?"

"On the bookcase in the living room."

"And you've looked in your room?"

"Yes. Well, not *everywhere* in my room."

"Let me see." Mrs. Dunn broke the egg into the mixing bowl and absent-mindedly licked her fingers. "Have you looked in the hall closet?

That's where your skates were last time you lost them."

"I'll look."

Danny hurried off. But the papers weren't in the closet.

After that, he tried all his usual "losing places" —the bottom drawer of his bureau, the old toy chest, now full of chemicals, the corner of the attic stair where he kept old electric motors— but the sentences were in none of them.

At last Mrs. Dunn asked, "Have you looked all through your pockets?"

"No," Danny said glumly. "I'm afraid to."

"Afraid—?"

"Because if the sentences aren't *there*, then I know they're really lost."

Mrs. Dunn couldn't help laughing. Then all at once she stopped. "Oh, dear," she said. "A dreadful thought just struck me. The Professor—!"

"What?"

"Well, Professor Bullfinch and Dr. Grimes left while you were eating breakfast. The Professor was arguing with Dr. Grimes about something, I don't remember what, but just before they left, he began looking through his pockets. He said,

'Wait a minute, I'll work out the equation for you if I can find some paper.' Now I just wonder—"

"Oh, Mom! I'll bet he took the sentences. He always writes on the backs of things." Danny held his head desperately. "Now what'll I do?"

Mrs. Dunn looked sympathetically at her son. "Oh, Danny. What a shame! If I'd only known."

Danny took a deep breath. "Well, there's one thing I know," he said. "I'm not going to write those sentences out again. Come on, Joe."

Mrs. Dunn asked, "Where are you going, Danny?"

"No place special."

"Hmm." Mrs. Dunn took Danny firmly by the arm and led him to one side. In a soft voice, so Joe couldn't hear, she said, "Don't act rashly, son. Joe mustn't know about—you know. And don't get in the Professor's way. You remember what day this is."

"Yes, Mom." Danny felt a twinge of guilt. This was hardly the time for him to go into a long explanation about Joe's discovery of the barn and its contents. He told himself that if his

77

mother knew about that, she would make no objections at all to their going together.

He kissed his mother good-by, and then he and Joe tore out of the house.

As they biked together up the Beckforth road, Joe asked, "You know what you told me yesterday? About the guards and everything? How will you get to the Professor?"

"Don't you remember?" Danny replied. "The culvert. We'll get into the barn without being stopped. Then, if I can just get hold of the Professor—"

He steered over to the side of the road. A jeep

was coming toward them. As it passed, they caught a glimpse of a tall, bronzed man in uniform sitting next to the driver.

"That's Colonel Beach, the pilot," Danny panted. "He must have just checked over the ship. I guess he'll be back soon. We'd better hurry or we'll miss the take-off. And—oh, gosh! —what if the Professor leaves my sentences in the ship?"

He pedaled faster than ever, and Joe had no breath left with which to answer him.

They left their bicycles in the woods on the other side of the stone wall, and Danny led the way. This time he went a roundabout way, through a boggy little hollow which ended in a grove of young willows. There was an earth

bank here, and in it the low stone archway of an old culvert, or drainage tunnel.

"The barn is just the other side of this hill," Danny whispered. "We'll have to crawl a little way."

He got down on his hands and knees and entered the culvert. Joe came right behind him.

The floor of the culvert was wet and slimy, and here and there water trickled from the roof and plopped on their heads or necks. They crawled along for what seemed like hours, although it was actually only a few minutes, and then they came into a gray patch of light. They were directly under the floor of the barn. Danny stopped. Above him was a grating. Behind him he could hear Joe mumbling faintly, "Trouble, trouble," and he grinned.

He reached up and pushed the grating aside. Cautiously he poked his head up. There, just a few paces away, was the great sphere of the ship, looking larger than it actually was. In the side facing Danny a round, open hatchway gaped.

As he watched, with his eyes on the level of the floor, Professor Bullfinch and Dr. Grimes walked briskly around the curve of the ship's side.

Danny heard the Professor saying, "—want to

show you the final arrangements for exterior viewing—"

They stepped through the hatchway and vanished inside the ship. But not before Danny had seen a familiar sheaf of yellow paper in the Professor's hand.

"Come on, Joe," he whispered. "They've gone into the ship. And he's got my sentences with him. I don't want to get caught now and put outside. We'll have to sprint for it."

A quick look around showed that the coast was clear. They scrambled up through the drain hole. A quick, short rush, and they tumbled through the hatchway and into the ship.

CHAPTER ELEVEN

An Unexpected View

They found themselves in a circular chamber with curving walls. A ladder led up through the middle of it. The ceiling was low, and the whole space was as snug and compact as a submarine control room.

On one wall were two neat bunks, one above the other. Next to them was a combination stove-and-refrigerator, with cupboards above and on either side of it. All these things were curved to fit the walls. On the far side was a thick window, at present shielded by steel plates. Beneath this was a control panel with several switches, colored buttons and dials, and a long red handle.

Joe tiptoed over to it.

"This must be where they'll run the ship from," he whispered. "What's this long handle? To steer it with?"

"No," Danny said. "You can't steer a space-ship that way." He had been inside the ship only

once before, but he couldn't resist showing Joe
how much he knew about it.

"I think," he said, taking hold of the lever,
"this opens and closes the hatch."

He pulled it a little way to the left, and glanced
over his shoulder. "Yes, the hatch is closed now.
See?"

"I see," said Joe with a shiver. "And I don't
like. Let it alone," he added, as Danny reached
for the lever again. "You might break something. Let's find Professor B. and get those sentences back."

"All right," said Danny. He went to the ladder. "The Professor and Dr. Grimes must be
up on the next deck. Come on."

He climbed the ladder like a monkey. Joe
went after him, muttering, "All I ever seem to
do is follow you around."

The next deck had an even lower ceiling, just
barely high enough for a man to stand up under.
A steel wall closed off part of it; the other, larger
part in which they stood consisted of long rows
of tanks. They were crowded with green plants
on racks, their roots deep in a solution of chemicals. Long ultraviolet tubes hung above
them.

As the boys stopped to stare at this curious gar-

83

den, a door in the wall opened and Dr. Grimes stepped through.

"Aha! What's this?" he cried.

Professor Bullfinch pushed past him through the small doorway. "Danny!" he said. "I'm surprised at you."

"Never mind him," said Dr. Grimes angrily. "Look at this. A snooper!"

He took two long steps and seized Joe by the collar.

"Who are you?" he barked. "What are you doing here? Don't try to lie to me!"

With each phrase he shook poor Joe so that his teeth clicked together, and he couldn't have answered if he had wanted to.

"Let him go," said the Professor. "He's only a boy."

"No matter," Grimes said. "This was supposed to be a top-secret project!"

"He's my friend," Danny protested.

Grimes glared. "I knew Willoughby was right."

"Just a minute, Grimes," Professor Bullfinch put in quietly. "Let go of the boy. I know Joe, and I'm sure there's some explanation."

Reluctantly, Dr. Grimes released his hold. Joe held his head with both hands.

"Oooh," he said, "you've shaken my brains into a malted milk."

"Well, Danny?" said the Professor patiently. "I am certain you didn't break your promise. How does it happen that Joe is here with you?"

Quickly Danny explained everything. "So you see," he finished, "I just had to get my sentences back, and since Joe already knew about the ship, we thought we'd watch the take-off too."

The Professor nodded. "I can't say that I blame you," he said. "It is most unfortunate. Are these your sentences?" He pulled the sheaf of paper from his pocket. "I'm sorry, I'm afraid the backs of them are covered with equations and sketches now."

Danny took the papers mournfully. "I'll have to do them again after all."

Professor Bullfinch sighed. "Well, as long as you're here, you may as well stay and watch the take-off."

Dr. Grimes was scowling. "Sentences!" he said scornfully, and from the way he looked at Joe it was clear he didn't altogether believe the story.

"Didn't you ever have to write out sentences when you were in school?" the Professor asked with a chuckle. "You must have been a model pupil. I had to write a hundred times, 'I will not contradict the teacher.' I had said that I thought it was possible to develop a speed faster than sound."

"Well, certainly I had to," Dr. Grimes said. "I was always in difficulties because of my rocket experiments. Once, in fact, I nearly blew up the high-school physics laboratory. But that doesn't excuse this sort of behavior."

In his heart Danny knew that Grimes was right, and it made him uncomfortable. So, to change the subject, he asked, "Can't you tell Joe a little about the ship, Professor? What's in there, through that door you just came out of?"

"Chiefly fuel for the rocket motors that will steer the ship. There's a ladder that leads to a small deck above in which are the heating-and-cooling plant, air-circulation motors, and so on. There are also additional supplies.

"This first flight," the Professor went on, "will only be to a height of two hundred miles. Colonel Beach and Major Baum will wear high-pressure suits in case of accident. They'll take the ship up and bring her down again. If nothing goes wrong, we'll have two or three more such trials, and then, eventually, they will try for the Moon."

"The Moon!" Joe exclaimed.

"Yes. The ship is fully supplied right now because we want to test the effect on food and plants as well as on the men. They are very brave men, believe me."

"Yes—and lucky too," Danny said enviously.

"Now let's go down to the main deck," said the Professor, "and I'll explain the living arrangements and the control panel to you. You know, Joe, Colonel Beach is named Joseph too. So one of the first human beings to see outer space will be a Joe."

"He can have it," Joe said fervently. "Not me. Not for a million dollars. I'm glad this Joe is staying right on the ground where, if you fall down, you can get up in one piece."

The Professor laughed and motioned to the boys to descend the ladder. When they were down, he and Dr. Grimes followed more slowly.

"This deck," he said, "as you can see, will be living quarters and ship control. Although there is a large window, most of the viewing will be done by television. There is a mobile TV camera with a speaker and microphone mounted on the outside of the hull, and a speaker, microphone, and screen in here. This is the two-way radio next to the control panel. With it they'll keep contact with the earth."

The Professor stopped abruptly and bent over

From the other three burst exclamations of
horror

the control panel. When he stood up again, he had an odd expression on his face.

"What's the trouble?" asked Dr. Grimes.

The Professor pointed to the hatchway. "Who shut that?" he asked.

The boys glanced at each other.

Danny said, "I was just showing Joe—"

The Professor bit his lip. Then, without another word, he punched a button on the control panel.

Slowly the steel shutters over the window slid back into grooves in the hull.

From the other three burst simultaneous exclamations of astonishment and horror. For outside the thick glass window were not the familiar walls of the barn but a few glittering stars in a vast dark-blue sky.

CHAPTER TWELVE

A Premature Party

"We are one hundred and twenty miles up!" said Professor Bullfinch in a solemn voice, pointing to a dial on the control panel.

The others stood frozen, unable to take their eyes from the window.

Then Danny burst out, "We're in space!"

"Not quite," said the Professor. "But we are one hundred miles higher than man has ever been before."

At that moment, Dr. Grimes cried hoarsely, "Shut it off. For heaven's sake, Bullfinch, stop the ship!" His voice cracked.

Professor Bullfinch swung toward him. The Professor's round face was pale behind his glasses, but he had lost none of his cheerful calm.

"Why?" he asked.

Dr. Grimes clenched his fists. "Why? Why? You fool, we'll be killed!" he shouted.

"Come to your senses, Grimes." The Professor's voice was coldly level, and it brought Dr. Grimes to a halt. "We haven't been killed yet.

Perhaps we won't be. On this first flight the ship was to go to two hundred miles. According to the altimeter, we've got eighty miles more. I say let's go on!"

His eyes were sparkling, and his courage and enthusiasm spread to Danny and Joe.

"Let's not be frightened of our shadows," he went on. "It was unfortunate that our take-off was an accident. But what is done is done."

He clasped his hands behind his back and turned to the window. The color of the sky was deepening, and more stars became visible every moment.

"I had no intention of being the pilot of this ship," said the Professor in a soft voice. "But now that I am, I can understand many things. I can understand why all our efforts have been bent toward getting out into space. Look at that —all the suns of the universe, and we are nearer to them than any man has ever been before."

At these words Dr. Grimes straightened his shoulders. His expression changed from fear to his usual sour frown. He moved to stand beside the Professor, and in a low tone he said, "You are right, Bullfinch. It is magnificent. I insist we go on."

"Good!" The Professor clapped his hands together. "First let's turn on the recording instruments. Grimes, you know where the panels are up above. Will you take care of them? I'll start the camera and the Geiger counter going."

He caught sight of Danny and Joe, huddled close together and not quite sure just how they felt. At once he came over to them.

"Danny," he said in a kindly voice, "you mustn't feel too bad about this. Even though you acted again without thinking, it may be all for the best. I must admit I'm having the time of my life."

"But I don't understand how it happened," Danny said. "All I did was shut the hatch with this lever."

"No. That lever charges the anti-gravity paint. As a safety measure, the hatch closes automatically when the power goes on."

He put his arms around both boys' shoulders. "You are a pair of good-for-nothing idiots," he said with a grin. "Let's forget it." He gave them an affectionate squeeze. "I'll turn on the television cameras, and you can take a look at the earth while I start some of the other instruments."

He snapped a switch and turned a dial. On one of the four screens mounted above the control panel a wonderful scene slowly took shape.

They could see the great curve of the earth's surface. They were much too high to see any details, but here and there great shining patches marked where the water lay, in contrast to the flat, darker land patches. Far to one side below a thick haze of air there was a gleaming band which the Professor told them was the sea.

"What are those little white spots below us?" Danny asked, pointing.

"Clouds," said the Professor. "We are twenty times higher than the highest mountain on earth. We are far above the clouds."

Joe swallowed. "Twenty times—! Ulp! You know," he said uneasily, "it's funny, but I feel seasick. Maybe it's looking at that ocean way over there—I never did like oceans—"

Danny said, "If Columbus could only have seen this, he could have saved himself a trip. The world *is* round!"

"But we fell off the edge," Joe said. "No, we didn't, we fell *up*. Oh, my head! How can you fall up?"

He staggered away from the screen and sat down on one of the bunks.

"How much longer will it take to get to the top?" he groaned.

"The top of what?" asked Danny. "There isn't any top."

"Oh, golly. No top—" Joe closed his eyes. "Well, how long before we get back to the bottom?"

"I don't know."

"It's already taken us all day to get this far up."

"What do you mean? We've only been flying for about an hour."

"But it's night," Joe said, pointing to the window.

"Oh, no," Danny said, laughing. "The air gets thinner and thinner as we go higher, and what we call blue sky is just the effect of the air on light waves. That's why the sky seems to be getting darker now and why we can see the stars. We're up where the air is thinned out."

Danny left his friend sitting on the bunk and went to watch the Professor, who was busily turning on various instruments, reading dials, and making notes.

"You know," Danny said, "it's a strange thing, but I feel very light somehow. Like I'm walking on air. Is it because we're up so high?"

"In a way, you *are* walking on air," the Professor replied. "The anti-gravity paint is shielding us from the earth's pull. Not altogether, since we haven't got it turned on full—luckily you didn't move that lever all the way over—but enough so that, as we go higher, our weight lessens."

Dr. Grimes came down the ladder. "What's the reading now?" he asked.

"One hundred and eighty-five miles." The Professor glanced at a dial. "At our present speed we have another seven or eight minutes."

"Fantastic!" Dr. Grimes looked at the television screen. "I still can't believe it. And without rockets—!"

The Professor grinned. Then he went to a cupboard above the stove and poked around in it for a moment or two. He brought out four bottles of ginger ale.

"Gentlemen," he said, looking around with twinkling eyes, "we are making history. I think the occasion calls for a little celebration. Let us drink a toast to the exploration of space."

He handed round the ginger ale and some straws.

"Danny," he said, "you have a lively mind. Can't you give us a song, or a poem, that will fit this moment?"

"Not me," said Danny. "Poetry is Joe's department. He's good at that."

Joe smiled bashfully; he was beginning to feel much better. He thought for a moment, and then he recited:

> I am a boy who has always thought it
> was quite a trip from home plate to
> first base,
> And now, all of a sudden, I find myself
> on the way to outer space;
> I can imagine myself zipped inside a
> leather briefcase
> Or in some even more unlikely place,
> But I find it hard to realize that I am on
> the way to outer space.
>
> I can picture myself as a contender in a
> three-legged race,
> Or as a movie star with a million-dollar
> face;
> In fact, just about the only way I cannot
> picture myself
> Is on the way to outer space.

He dropped his eyes modestly as the other three applauded.

The Professor raised his bottle

Professor Bullfinch said, "Do you mind if I set that to music?"

"Oh, come on," Joe mumbled. "Quit kidding."

"No, really, Joe, it was very good indeed." The Professor raised his bottle. "To our excellent bard. Drink up."

They drank, and he added, "Grimes, watch the altimeter and speed dials. I'm about to cut down the current."

He took hold of the red lever. Grimes bent over the control board.

"Oh-ten," he began counting. "Oh-nine, oh-eight, oh-seven—"

The Professor pushed the handle a little way toward the right.

"—oh-three," said Grimes, "oh-two, oh-one, zero. Two hundred miles, Bullfinch."

The Professor slowly drew the red lever farther over.

"That's it," he said decisively. He glanced through the window. "Our trip is over. But it was a magnificent, an unforgettable—"

He broke off.

At the same time Dr. Grimes clutched the edge of the control panel with both hands and shouted, "Bullfinch! There's something wrong!"

The Professor stared at the dials. Then he grabbed the lever and jerked it all the way to the right.

"No good!" Dr. Grimes fairly screamed. "We're going faster than ever—away from the earth!"

CHAPTER THIRTEEN

Broken Speech

"Help!" yelled Joe. "Let me out of here!"

Danny caught his friend's arm. "Stop it," he hissed. "Quit acting like a baby."

Joe looked at him with wide eyes. Then he was silent, except for the chattering of his teeth. Dr. Grimes had sunk down into the pilot's seat and was holding his head between his hands. Only Professor Bullfinch seemed in command of himself.

"Keep calm, all of you," he said in a strong voice. "Grimes, I'm ashamed of you. Is this how a scientist should act? Look at Danny."

Grimes lifted a haggard face. "Danny!" he snarled. "Yes, look at him! It's his fault, the whole thing!"

Danny bit his lip. "You're right," he said. "I'm—I'm to blame. I don't know what to—"

The Professor interrupted him. "It no longer matters who's to blame. Let's try to find out what's wrong and get it fixed."

Grimes simply moaned. "What hope is there?"

"I don't know yet. But whether we like it or not, we are the crew of this ship. Let's act like crewmen."

He turned toward the boys with a smile. Danny said, "We're ready. Tell us what to do." He nudged Joe, who nodded, still unable to talk.

"Good," said the Professor. "You know something about radio, Dan. Get on the set and see if you can make contact with our base."

Delighted at the chance to act, Danny sprang to the radio. The Professor, seeing that Joe needed something to keep his mind off their predicament, set him to watch the television screen. By that time Dr. Grimes had pulled himself together, and he and the Professor began to check over the lever mechanism.

From where he sat at the radio Danny could see the observation port. Consequently, he was the first to see a round silver globe swing into view. The receiver broke into wild peeps and squeals.

"Professor!" he shouted. "Look! We've reached the Moon!"

Professor Bullfinch ran to the window. "The

Moon? Nonsense, Danny. You should recognize that," he said. "It's the satellite."

Danny stared. Now he remembered it: the bright metal sphere with antennas poking out of two sides. It seemed years since that day he had peered at it through the Professor's telescope. In a way, that had been the start of this whole adventure.

He bent over the radio again. And suddenly a voice came through the speaker:

"—which at first was thought to be an enemy missile and then a flying saucer, is now revealed to be an experimental spaceship, the government announced a few minutes ago.

"The ship, which is believed to operate on a secret principle developed by Professor Euclid Bullfinch of Midston University, took off unexpectedly at 10:20 A.M. without a pilot. However, the inventor and Dr. A. J. Grimes of the International Rocket Society may be aboard. We'll bring you further bulletins as they come in."

Joe said, "Hey! They didn't even mention us."

"Never mind the news," said the Professor. "Keep trying to reach the base, Dan."

Danny flipped the broadcast switch once more.

"Hello! Mr. Willoughby! Mr. Willoughby! Come in, Mr. Willoughby!"

He snapped the switch again. Almost at once a voice said sharply, "It's about time you called. Bullfinch! Are you there?"

The Professor leaned over Danny's shoulder and said into the microphone, "Willoughby, this is Bullfinch. We're in trouble."

"You bet you are!" Mr. Willoughby replied. "Washington is seething. But that's the least of it. I have two hysterical mothers on my hands right here. Now, what's it all about?"

In a few hasty words Professor Bullfinch explained to the startled project head how they had happened to take off so abruptly and why they couldn't return.

"I see," said Mr. Willoughby. "Stand by, Bullfinch. I'll get Colonel Beach. Maybe he—" He stopped. Then they heard him say, "Madam, please!" There was a scuffling sound. "Madam! No! Ouch!"

A woman's voice in the speaker said, "Joe! Joseph! Are you all right?"

Joe gasped, "It's my mother."

"Joe!" said his mother's voice. "Answer me this minute!"

103

Danny snapped the switch and pushed Joe in front of the microphone.

"Y-y-yes," Joe said. "I'm all right. I'm fine, Ma."

"I phoned your father. He'll be here soon, and he'll take care of everything. Oh, Joe—why did you do it?"

Joe looked helplessly at Danny. "But it wasn't *my* fault. Honest, Ma!"

Then Mrs. Dunn's voice cut in. "Danny?"

"Yes, Mom?" Danny said, his throat closing at the sound of his mother's worried tone.

"Danny, take care of yourself. I can't talk long—here comes Colonel Beach. I know you'll be all right, darling, with the Professor there. Oh, Danny—be careful!"

"I will, Mom," Danny said.

Then they heard a deep voice say, "This is Beach. What's wrong, Professor Bullfinch?"

The Professor replied, "I'm not sure. Unfortunately neither Grimes nor I are mechanics or electricians. We are both physicists."

"Well, Professor, can you describe to me exactly what happened?" asked Colonel Beach.

The Professor did so and gave him the readings of the various instruments.

"Sounds to me," the Colonel said when the

Professor had finished, "as if maybe your power relay is stuck. That's the switch that relays power from the solar battery through the anti-gravity paint. Tell you what. Set your TV camera on the upper track. You'll be able to see the relay just below the battery housing. Then try switching your power down. If the relay doesn't move, that may be it. Check it and get back to me. Meantime I'll try to figure out how you can fix it without going outside the ship."

The Professor and Dr. Grimes did as he suggested. Watching the television screen, they could see the little relay. The Professor moved the lever. The switch remained motionless.

"That's it, then," the Professor said.

They looked with relief and joy at each other.

Joe muttered, "Unless it's something else too," but nobody paid any attention to him.

"We'll be home soon," said the Professor. "Dan, let me get at the radio."

He snapped the sending switch. "Colonel Beach! This is Bullfinch. You were right—it was the relay. It didn't— Oops!"

Without warning his feet had left the deck. His body floated out horizontally like a banner in the wind.

Startled, he kicked frantically to right himself.

The Professor shot backward like a torpedo

Instead he shot forward. He put out a hand to steady himself, and his hand went right through the speaker of the radio. There was a crash.

The Professor shot backward through the air like a torpedo. And after him came floating a cloud of little pieces of metal and glass—the fragments of broken radio tubes.

CHAPTER FOURTEEN

"They Float through the Air"

Dr. Grimes gave a strangled cry. He was drifting in the air between the Professor and the hopelessly broken radio. At the same time Joe with a yell went sailing up off the floor.

Danny had been holding the back of the pilot's seat. He stared at the others. Then he reached up to pull Joe down. At once he too drifted up from the deck, slowly turned upside down, and hung helpless in midair.

Professor Bullfinch was the first to recover.

"I fear," he said, brushing aside a few small bits of radio that floated before his face, "we'll never learn whether Beach figured out a way to fix the relay."

Joe, who was hanging near the ceiling, said in a shaking voice, "I'm dead. I'm an angel."

"Not quite yet, Joe," said the Professor. "We are simply completely free of the earth's gravity. To all intents and purposes we simply don't weigh anything."

Joe felt himself nervously. "I guess you're

right." He looked down at the deck, eight feet below him, and groaned. "But I don't know," he said. "Maybe being dead would be easier."

Dr. Grimes growled, "Don't worry. We'll all be dead soon enough. Well, Bullfinch, what do you propose to do about this?"

At this Danny broke in. "Yes, before you do anything else, why don't you all get right side up?"

The Professor looked at him and chuckled. "I have news for you, Danny," he said. "You're the one who's upside down. That is, if there can be said to be any *right* side up where there's no gravity."

"But—but—" Danny stammered, "I don't feel upside down."

"That's partly because without gravity the blood cannot rush to your head, nor can you orient yourself. Just a minute."

The Professor began to make awkward swimming motions and succeeded in thrashing his way over to a locker. Hanging on to the door handle with one hand, he fished out a pair of boots with magnetic soles. He struggled into them, and at once his feet swung down and clicked against the metal deck. He took out another pair and handed them to Grimes. Then he reached up, took hold of the boys, and fished them down out of the air.

"You'll have to learn how to pull yourselves around by handholds," he said. "There are only two pairs of boots, and I'm afraid they were made for men, not boys. For the time being hang on to the edge of the table. Grimes, are you all right?"

"I'm all right in an all-wrong sort of way," Grimes puffed angrily. He clumped to a chair and sat down. Danny now noticed for the first time that all the furniture was bolted to the deck, and he understood why.

"We had better hold a council of war," the Professor said, sitting down at the head of the table.

Danny tried to smile, although he was feeling far from happy. Part of his misery came as a result of hearing his mother's voice and realizing just how far away she was. And part of it was a sense of guilt that all this was his fault and his alone.

The Professor said, "I can see that our two junior members are feeling better. Now, let's face the facts. At this moment I don't know where we're going or how we're ever going to get back. I do know this, however: as a scientist I'm not afraid."

He paused and looked round at the others. Then he said solemnly, "The unknown is not to be feared, but studied. If this is to be the end, I intend to see and learn all I can before I die. But to waste time in worry is useless and unscientific. And death is itself only one more experience for a scientist."

Dr. Grimes frowned. "Bullfinch," he said, "if you are implying that I'm wasting time, you're wrong. I'll admit I was a little startled, that's all."

The Professor smiled. "Fine. I don't know what I'd do if you weren't ready to argue with me and keep me on my toes."

Joe said slowly, "I don't seem to be as scared as I was. I guess I'm getting used to it."

"How do you feel, Danny?" the Professor asked.

"Oh, I'm all right." Danny sighed. "Only I wish there was something I could do to—to make up for getting you into this mess."

"There is," said the Professor gently. "Forget about it. We have too many other things to do."

"Yes, sir," Danny said almost in a whisper.

"Well, then, we're all squared away. We'll have to plan a routine and assign jobs. To begin with, suppose you and Joe get some dinner ready. Dr. Grimes, why don't you try to figure roughly what our course is? There's an automatic course plotter into which you can feed data. I'll get to work on the relay and see if I can think of some way to repair it."

The two boys quickly learned how to handle themselves in the absence of gravity. They found they could get about quickly by shoving against walls or decks with their feet or hands and shooting through the air. They also learned to hook their toes under open drawers or chair seats when they wanted to stand still, for the slightest push would send them drifting off.

It was like their dreams of flying come true. They never tired of the games they could play zipping through the air from place to place. And when they were tired, they found there was nothing more pleasant than to lie still, floating like thistledown on the faint air currents that moved through the ship.

They had a little difficulty at first with the food. They could slice solid things like cheese and meat, but they had to handle them with care.

112

Dan and Joe swam after them

Putting a sandwich down too hard would cause it to float away in separate pieces.

At one point Joe tried to pour some milk out of a container. Instead of pouring, it dropped out in round white globules which went bouncing like bubbles all over the cabin. Dan and Joe swam after them through the air, but when they tried to catch one it bounded away and broke into a number of even smaller bubbles.

"What we need for this," Joe panted, "is a butterfly net. How are we going to drink this stuff?"

"Not too difficult," said the Professor, looking up from his work. "We'll simply trap one in a glass and stick a straw into it. Sucking and swallowing don't depend on gravity."

Joe managed at last to assemble the pieces of milk in a container. Danny meantime had opened a package of cheese, but as he held it down on the table, the knife went sailing away. He reached into his pants pocket and fished out his own knife. But the handle caught in his pocket lining, and the pocket turned inside out. The next instant the air was full of a strange assortment of things from his pocket, and Danny dropped everything in a wild attempt to get them back.

The Professor glanced up in surprise as a pencil missed his nose by an inch.

"Dear me," he said. "Is the storeroom leaking?"

Joe dodged a marble and swam through the air to the galley. He got a strainer and began scooping objects in. Eventually everything was rounded up.

Professor Bullfinch came over to watch Danny putting his treasures away. As he stowed them in his pocket, the Professor ticked them off on his fingers.

"String, a pencil stub, two nails, five paper clips, a marble, a piece of wire, a used pipe cleaner. I ought to make a study of the expandable nature of boys' pockets," he said. "What's this?"

"It's a watch spring," Danny explained. "It's useful too. I read once that a man cut his way out of jail with one."

"I see. I hope you never have to use it. And what's this odd coin?"

"Oh, Miss Arnold once gave me that. It's a lempira from Honduras. I keep it because I like the name."

"And this?"

"Well, that's a jingle from a cowboy spur. And this thing is the inside of a radio tube."

"Heavens! I'm out of fingers," said the Professor. "And here's an old cough drop. At least, I think it's a cough drop."

"Yes. That's in case I'm ever hungry."

"I see. And what is this thing?" the Professor finished, holding up a flat piece of plastic.

Danny scratched his head. "I don't remember what it is," he said, "but it must be good for something, or I'd have thrown it away."

"That is quite a collection," the Professor said. "Please don't turn out any other pockets if you can help it."

Danny grinned. "I know. Sometimes I'm afraid to put my hands in my pockets, because I never know *what* I'll find."

Dr. Grimes, who had been bending over the pilot's table paying no attention to what was going on, now turned around.

"Bullfinch," he said, "I've got our course worked out."

"Ah! Where are we heading?"

Dr. Grimes passed a weary hand over his eyes. When he spoke, it was to say only one word: "Mars."

116

CHAPTER FIFTEEN

Bounced!

Danny finished checking over the cases of food and straightened up with a long sigh. It was some weeks since they had gone flying off the earth, and he had found that you could get used to living in a spaceship—even one heading for the mystery of another planet.

As they drew closer and closer to Mars, each took turns watching the planet through the ship's telescope. The rest of each day was given over to the chores of keeping house, and the two boys spent a certain amount of time in instruction on operating the different instruments and in classes given by both the Professor and Dr. Grimes in mathematics, astronomy, chemistry, and physics. The two men also spent a good deal of time trying to get the relay working again, but without success.

One of Danny's jobs was the daily check of the supplies so that they could plan which foods to ration. The problem of food had been made a little easier by the existence of the air-supply garden, where they raised Dr. Grimes's roses as well as green vegetables and some fruits.

Danny closed the door of the storeroom behind him. In the garden there was a steamy green smell. Professor Bullfinch was bending over some plants in a tank, looking very curious indeed because he now had quite a full beard.

"Ouch!" he exclaimed as Danny flew in. "I wish we could grow thornless roses."

"Why don't you wear gloves?" Danny suggested.

"It's not my hands but my beard I'm talking about. It gets tangled in the thorns." He straightened up. "I wish we'd brought a razor along. But then, I didn't plan so long a stay in the ship."

Danny smiled wanly. "It sure is different from what I used to daydream. I used to make up stories about rocket flight and fighting enemies on other planets—and here we are, fighting roses and doing mathematics."

The Professor looked shrewdly at him. "Something's troubling you, my boy," he said. "What is it?"

Danny caught hold of a loop of rope; they had tied a number of them in various places to serve as handholds.

"Well, you know," he said, stumbling a little over the words, "it's—it's my fault. The whole thing, I mean. Whenever I look at Joe, I can't help thinking—he never wanted to take a trip into space. I got him into this. And I can't get him out again."

The Professor stroked his beard. "Hm. Yes, you did get him into this. And he's lucky to have you for a friend. So am I, as a matter of fact."

Danny raised his head. "What? Why do you say that?"

"If it weren't for you, my boy, we might not have discovered the anti-gravity paint in the first place. Your hasty action which knocked over the beaker led to this."

"Oh," said Danny. "I never thought of that."

"Well, it's so. I think you've learned your lesson. You must think ahead and plan carefully if you want to be a scientist. But on the other hand, there are times when a scientist must be prepared to jump into things—to take chances. It doesn't hurt to be a *little* headstrong. Sometimes a man like me needs a boy like you to push him into things."

Danny's spirits rose for the first time in days. He looked with wide eyes into the Professor's smiling face.

"Yes," he said. "I see. But—but what about Dr. Grimes? He doesn't want me to push him—"

"What about Dr. Grimes?" The rocket expert's stern face, looking even sterner for its iron-gray beard, appeared almost at their feet as he climbed the ladder. He hoisted himself up and clicked his magnetic shoes firmly to the deck.

"I heard what you said," Grimes went on. "I have been meaning to say this for some time." He paused, frowning, and Danny felt himself growing limp again with nervousness.

Then Grimes barked, "I am deeply grateful to you, young man, for giving me this opportunity to be one of the first men in space. It's certainly true that I would never have done this myself. But although it was a regrettable accident, I am glad of it!"

He cleared his throat. "As President of the International Rocket Society," he said, "it gives me pleasure to make you an honorary life member of the Society."

And with that he removed the little gold rocket pin from the lapel of his jacket, reached up to where Danny hung, and fastened it to the front of the boy's shirt.

120

Danny drew a long breath. "Gee! Thanks!" he said. "And Joe too?"

"Yes," said Dr. Grimes, "Joe too."

At that precise moment Joe, who was on watch and unaware of the honor he had just received, hailed them from his post at the telescope.

"Professor! Dr. Grimes! Come quick!"

The two scientists clambered down the ladder. When they were clear, Danny dove down head-first.

Joe was clinging to a rope loop at the eyepiece of the telescope. "A message!" he was shouting. "A message from Mars!"

"The boy's gone mad!" said Dr. Grimes.

"Calm down, Joe," the Professor said. "Tell us what you mean."

"Well, I was watching that big green patch—you know. I saw a little flashing light. I didn't think anything about it until I saw that it was flashing regularly—on, off, on, off, like Morse code."

Dr. Grimes snorted. "That would mean," he said, "that a thinking being was signaling to us. Anyone who has read my book on Mars knows that's impossible."

"I read it," the Professor said mildly. "Hm—"

121

Danny meanwhile had been looking into the telescope. He said, "I don't see any light, Joe. Where is it?"

"Aha! You see?" Dr. Grimes was triumphant. "It was probably a reflection from the polar icecap."

"But regular flashes—" the Professor began.

"Nonsense! The boy's head is full of science-fiction novels," said Grimes.

Danny was once more peering through the telescope. Since they had come close to Mars— they were within seven thousand miles by now— he never tired of the exciting view. Even without the telescope, through the view port, they could see the vast greenish-red curve with the bright white patch of snow near the bottom and great areas of green that were possibly plants. The telescope showed the shadows of low, rolling mountain ranges and wide, irregular dark lines that might have been deep gorges twenty times larger than the Grand Canyon. Now and then across the red-brown spaces that were deserts he could see yellow dust clouds or sand storms whirling. He and Joe had watched in fascination; another planet, another world, strange beyond measure, and yet so like their own familiar earth in some ways. Many times they had discussed the question of life on Mars and what it might be like.

Suddenly he squinted more attentively into the eyepiece. Yes—there it was! A tiny blink of light, no brighter than a match in the middle of the Sahara Desert—once again, and yet again!

"Professor!" he gasped. "Look! I see it!"

Professor Bullfinch took a step forward. Then he said, "Let Dr. Grimes look. He is the most unbiased of us."

Dr. Grimes pursed his lips and went to the telescope. While they stood breathless, he looked into it.

"I don't see a thing," he said at last.

"Let me see," the Professor said.

He took off his glasses and polished them carefully. He put his hands on his knees and bent forward. He put his eye to the eyepiece.

"Well?" said Grimes impatiently.

"Do you see it?" Danny cried.

"Amazing," said the Professor.

Joe was biting his fingernails. "What is it?" Danny fairly screamed.

"Eh? Why, an eclipse," the Professor replied. "Very interesting indeed. The moon has passed between the surface of the planet and ourselves. I can't see the planet at all."

"The moon!" Joe said in surprise. "I thought you showed us Mars's moon this morning about seven thousand miles back."

"That was Deimos," said the Professor. "Mars has two moons. This one which is between Mars and ourselves is called Phobos. We'll have to wait ten or fifteen minutes to see the surface again. By then perhaps it'll be somewhat clearer."

Dr. Grimes glanced at the control panel. "I'm afraid not," he said.

"No? Why?"

Dr. Grimes pointed to one of the dials. "We have bounced!"

"Bounced?"

"Exactly. We had come to within 7,075 miles. Just now, as I looked, the needle began rising again. We are now at 7,089 miles and rapidly getting farther away."

Professor Bullfinch took his lower lip between thumb and forefinger. "Hm. Then our anti-gravity paint actually causes us to be bounced away from an object's mass?"

"Just so. The approach of Phobos gave us a little additional push, as it were."

"An eclipse!"

"Too bad," said the Professor. "I had hoped to come closer to Mars."

Dr. Grimes bent over the course plotter. "We are heading into outer space again," he said.

The Professor sighed. "Now we'll have to wait for our next trip to find out if you're right, Grimes. About life on Mars, I mean."

Dr. Grimes slowly shook his head. "We're bouncing further away from the sun," said he. "There may not be another trip for us."

CHAPTER SIXTEEN

One More Chance

Red, sandy Mars had faded behind them. The spaceship crossed the path of giant Jupiter and flew toward the sixth planet—Saturn. Its bright disk, surrounded by the broad band of its rings, loomed larger in the view port every day. They could see streaks of yellow and tan on its liquid surface, boiling clouds of gases, and an enormous dark stripe that was the shadow cast by its rings.

The Professor and Dr. Grimes were busy hour after hour, calculating their probable course if they should bounce away again.

"There's not much doubt that we'll bounce," Professor Bullfinch said. "The question is: which way?"

"Why is that so important?" Danny wanted to know.

The Professor pointed to a chart of the solar system. "To put it in its simplest terms, if we bounce this way, we'll head toward the earth again. That will give us one more chance to get that switch working and get home. If we bounce that way, we'll fly out still farther from the sun. We won't cross the paths of any other planets. Eventually, since there will be nothing to stop us or bounce us back again, we'll be so far away that we'll freeze to death."

The next few days were full of tension. All four of them went about their work quietly. No one could think of anything but "Which way? Which way?" And always Saturn came closer and closer.

There came the moment at last, with all of them clustered around the pilot's table. Saturn was so huge that, although they were a hundred thousand miles from it, it filled the entire port. They could see swirling masses of pink on its yellow-orange surface, which, the Professor said, was less dense than water for all its size.

Nervous sweat beaded the foreheads of the two scientists as they sat in their shirt sleeves hunched over the table. They checked the readings of various dials and jotted down equations on the pads before them.

Dr. Grimes threw down his pencil. "We're slowing. We are reaching the crucial point—the 'bounce zone.'"

Everyone looked at the distance indicator,

And always Saturn came closer and closer

which in a few moments might signal life or death.

Danny, hardly knowing he was doing so, began counting as their speed diminished, reading the figures in thousands of miles per hour from the dial: "Ten, nine, eight, seven—"

Joe closed his eyes as if bracing himself for a shock.

"Six, five, four, three—"

The Professor gripped the edge of the table.

"—two, one, zero!"

There was a second of dreadful silence.

Slowly the needle on the dial began to rise again.

The Professor said huskily, "Here we go."

He bent over the automatic course plotter, which was clucking like a hen. He began adjusting the knobs on the front which fed data into it.

Dr. Grimes and the Professor stared at the tape which emerged. Then they looked at each other. With a groan Dr. Grimes turned away. The Professor sighed and slowly lowered himself into the pilot's seat.

Joe said, "I knew it, I knew it. The wrong way —huh?"

The Professor nodded.

Danny clung to a loop of rope, speechless. All

he could think of at this awful moment was the mockery of his old daydreams. He had played spaceship with such a light heart. And here he was, millions of miles from home, heading with his companions into the vast emptiness of space, with nothing ahead but death from the bitter cold.

He looked at the view port. Saturn's giant disk grew visibly smaller as he watched. Never had the planet seemed so alien and strange, and yet he thought to himself, "That may be the last familiar thing I'll ever see."

Then he blinked. Was it his imagination? The thick quartz glass of the port was glowing red.

He rubbed his eyes. The glare increased until the port shone like a dozen sunsets.

Danny came to his senses. "Fire!" he yelled.

Every head jerked up.

"The ship's on fire! We're melting!" he babbled.

The Professor looked at the port and sprang to his feet.

"What in heaven—" he began.

"We're not on fire, nor are we melting," Grimes put in. "It's a reflection. Something is approaching us from the side."

He snapped on the TV camera. One of the screens lit up.

Both Danny and Joe yelped involuntarily. A blazing ball of gas almost filled the screen.

"A comet!" the Professor exclaimed.

"And we are near its path," Dr. Grimes added.

"Wh-wh-what'll happen if it hits us?" asked Joe.

"That depends," said the Professor. "A comet's head is mainly chunks of meteoric material which give off flaming gas. Its tail is composed of gas and dust particles as well. If the head should pass within a hundred miles of us, we might be boiled alive. If the tail alone comes near—well, I don't know—"

Danny said, "Shouldn't we close the shutters?"

"By all means. The light might blind us."

Danny touched the control, and the steel shutters closed tight over the port. Even so, the light from the TV screen was dazzling.

"Close your eyes," the Professor commanded.

They did so. Even through closed lids the glare penetrated, although the comet was thousands of miles away. Faintly they could hear a hissing, crackling sound like a distant forest fire.

Then slowly the glare died. Hardly daring to believe that the danger had passed, they looked up again. The screen was dark once more, save for a pale luminosity like shining dust.

In a trembling voice Dr. Grimes said, "We must have passed close to the edge of the tail—perhaps within two thousand miles."

From the automatic course plotter there came a sudden steady clicking, as if the machine, in relief at their narrow escape, were chuckling happily.

"Something's wrong," said Danny.

The Professor stared at the tape. Then he looked round at the others with a radiant smile. "No!" he chortled. "Something's right!"

"What?" said Grimes.

"Yes. The comet has changed our course. We have one more chance to fix that relay. We're heading back toward the earth!"

CHAPTER SEVENTEEN

Danny Wakes the Ship

Dinner was over, and they were still sitting around the table. The boys were tied to their seats as usual, for comfort's sake. The Professor and Dr. Grimes were sipping coffee out of sealed plastic bottles. Joe was munching a piece of chocolate.

The Professor said, "Well, let's go over it again. We are very close to what we've called the bounce zone. Whatever we do we must do within the next ten hours, before we get to the point at which the earth's gravity will bounce us away again.

"We've tried banging against the inside of the hull to jar the relay loose. No good. We can't get ouside because we haven't any space suits. The outside wiring is a separate circuit from that inside, and works off the solar battery. I can't think of anything else."

Dr. Grimes folded his arms. "What about the rockets? We have a belt of rocket exhausts all round the outside of the ship for steering. If our momentum carries us close enough, we can use the rockets to force ourselves into the earth's atmosphere. The heat of the friction may loosen the switch."

"Yes. It may also burn up the ship, however," said the Professor.

"It's a chance we ought to take. I'm surprised at you, Bullfinch. Didn't I hear you telling young Dan that a scientist must sometimes be daring?"

"Quite true. I'm not saying that we shouldn't try that. I'm just wondering what our chances of survival are."

"Rubbish!" Dr. Grimes banged the table with his fist. "The fact is, you just don't like rockets. You've got yourself single-tracked on anti-gravity."

"Don't be silly, Grimes. In the first place, I don't think we can come close enough to the atmosphere—"

There was an empty jam jar with a magnetic metal base on the table. They had filled it with roses to give the rather severe-looking cabin a more homey air. As the two scientists argued and as Dr. Grimes went on banging the table with his fist, this jar jumped slightly and began to slide toward the edge of the table.

Danny was the only one who noticed it. He

didn't think about it until it got to the very edge. Just then Dr. Grimes shouted, "Fiddlesticks! I'm sure that a blast from all the rockets on one side—"

He gave the table a heavy bang. The jar leaped and went off the edge.

"Watch it!" Danny cried, and made a grab for the jar. He missed. The jar dropped to the deck, where its magnetic base clamped it fast. But the air was filled with roses and blobs of water. The argument ended as the scientists and the boys dodged floating water drops and chased the thorny roses.

Later, when everyone had gone to bed, Danny found himself unable to sleep. He tossed and turned in the air, drifting about at the end of his cord, restless and uncomfortable.

There had been something in that scene between the Professor and Dr. Grimes that almost seemed to him as if it had happened before: the two of them arguing, and a vase falling and breaking. . . .

Then suddenly it came to him. Of course! They had been playing music together at home, long ago. A vase had fallen off the sideboard. His mother had come running in and they had argued about how it had happened.

He thought of his mother. What was she

doing now, he wondered. Worrying about him, maybe weeping, keeping his things for him just as they had been when he left . . .

He had a vivid image of his own room at home, of all the familiar things, of his mother saying, "It will be hard, but we'll get you to college, Danny." College! He wondered whether he'd ever see home again, whether they'd ever be all together

again in those familiar scenes—the Professor with his bull fiddle, Dr. Grimes with his little piccolo, making music, all comfortable and happy and snug . . .

And suddenly he came wide awake. "Hey!" he said aloud. "That's it!"

A moment later he had snapped on the lights and was shouting, "Professor Bullfinch! Dr. Grimes! Wake up! I've got it! I know how we can loosen the switch!"

139

CHAPTER EIGHTEEN

More Music

The Professor awoke with a start. Automatically he unbuckled his safety belt, and went sailing out of bed so swiftly that he bumped his head.

"What?" he gasped. "What's happened?"

He caught a loop of rope to steady himself. "What on earth is the matter?"

"I've got it!" Danny cried. "Vibrations!"

The Professor shook his head to clear it and rubbed his eyes. "You've got vibrations? Where?"

"I mean I know how we can shake the switch loose. I've got an idea," Danny said.

"Oh, Dan!" said the Professor, and there was a hint of exasperation in his voice. "I thought something had happened to you. For heaven's sake, boy, when will you ever learn—"

Dr. Grimes, sitting up in his bunk, snapped, "This is the last straw. Throw him out the air lock! Now he won't even let us sleep."

"But listen!" Danny yelled. "Give me a chance to explain!"

The Professor took a deep breath. "Dan," he said, "I think I have been very patient with you. But now—"

Danny kicked against the wall and sent himself shooting toward the table. He caught hold of the edge of it.

"Please," he begged. "Listen to me. That jam jar. When Dr. Grimes banged the table, the vibrations of his banging made it slide off the edge—isn't that so? Just like that time when you and he were playing music, and the vibrations of the piccolo made that vase fall and break. Why couldn't we do the same thing to the switch?"

The two scientists stared at him. Then Dr. Grimes said, "It wasn't the piccolo. But maybe you've got a point."

"By George!" said the Professor. "You mean shake the switch loose with a high note from a musical instrument? Danny, my boy—this is certainly worth thinking about."

He propelled himself awkwardly into his bunk and struggled into his magnetic shoes. Dr. Grimes already had his on and was clumping about enthusiastically. Joe, wakened by the noise at last, yawned enormously and asked, "What's going on? Have we landed?"

141

He joined the others sitting at the table and added, "I knew there was something about this trip I didn't like: I forgot to bring a toothbrush."

The Professor said, "In the first place, how could we get outside to play a note at the switch?"

"I've already thought of that," Danny said proudly. "The TV would do. We've got a speaker on the outside of the hull along with the cameras, and a mike in here. We can use the controls to set the speaker near the switch."

"That's right!" the Professor exclaimed, beaming. "You've really worked it all out."

"Hm!" Dr. Grimes sniffed. "Only one thing's been forgotten. We haven't got one of your vibrating bull fiddles, Bullfinch."

The Professor tugged at his beard. "We can make one," he answered. "The body and neck could be made of wood from some of the supply cases. The bow could be made of heavy-gauge wire, bent into shape."

"What would you string the fiddle with?" Dr. Grimes asked.

"All we need is one string—the higher in pitch the better, perhaps. A violin E-string is fine aluminum wire; I'm sure we have some somewhere on the ship."

"Yes, but won't we need horsehair on the bow?" said Grimes.

Joe yawned. "How about using your beards for that?" he suggested.

They looked at him in surprise. "Why, Joe! What a good idea!" said the Professor.

"Oh, it was nothing," Joe said modestly. "It probably won't work anyway."

Full of enthusiasm, they went to work at once. Dr. Grimes broke up a packing case, and Danny and Joe, using small nails from one of Danny's pockets, put together a rough square box with a hole in the front. To one end they fastened a long slat. A skate key from another pocket made a good peg with which to tighten the string, which the Professor made from some fine wire. Dr. Grimes bent heavier wire into the proper shape for the bow, and the Professor found, again in one of Danny's pockets, a piece of his own bull-fiddle rosin.

"We need a bridge too," he said.

"What's that?" Danny asked.

"Something to hold the string up off the body of the instrument."

"Oh." Danny fished thoughtfully in his pockets again.

"Would this do?" He brought out a flat, strangely shaped piece of plastic. "I told you it might be good for something."

The Professor and Dr. Grimes cut several hairs

from their beards, and in a surprisingly short time the "space fiddle," as the Professor called it, was ready.

They waited until their instruments told them they were almost at the "bounce zone." Then Dr. Grimes sat down before the knobs which controlled the position of the TV camera and microphone on the outside of the hull. Danny and Joe held on to loops of rope and watched the screen. Carefully Dr. Grimes maneuvered the outside speaker until it was only a few inches away from the switch. In the screen they could clearly see the plastic housing which covered the relay. Many times in the past months they had stared hopelessly at it, wishing they could somehow get to it. Now, each of them felt, this was really the last chance—the last time they might look at the simple little device on which their lives hung.

The Professor turned the control lever of the ship to the "off" position. He sat down and placed the space fiddle between his knees. Experimentally he drew the bow across the string. There was a long-drawn-out screech.

"Ow!" Joe said. "That went right through my head!"

Danny gritted his teeth and kept his eyes on the screen.

There was a long-drawn-out screech

"Put the volume up a little, Grimes," said the Professor.

Dr. Grimes did so. The Professor turned the skate key and tightened the wire string. Once more he drew the bow across it.

Danny shuddered. The noise was so awful that he felt his teeth were jarring loose. The image on the TV screen wavered as if static were going through it.

Joe said, "Must be a plane going overhead. Oops! No, I forgot."

The Professor gave the key another half turn and played another note.

"Great heavens!" Dr. Grimes moaned. "I can't stand much more of this."

"It moved!" Danny shouted. "That time I saw it! It really moved!"

"I can't turn the key much more," gasped Professor Bullfinch. "I'm afraid the wire will snap."

Once again he played a long, dreadful note: SCREECH!

Once again their hair stood on end, and shivers ran down their backbones. The sound was exactly like that of someone scraping a piece of chalk over a blackboard—only shriller, higher, and more piercing.

SCREECH!

146

"Look!" Danny cried at the top of his voice. Pla-a-anggg! The wire snapped.

And at the same time, in the screen, they saw the relay pop open.

The neck of the space fiddle broke off. The clumsy, crudely made body flew apart.

"Ouch!" said Professor Bullfinch as the wire hit him across the fingers.

The air was full of drifting pieces of wood, fragments of wire, strands of beard, and nails. Then slowly everything began to settle to the floor. Both Danny and Joe felt themselves growing heavier. They sank down through the air until their feet touched the deck.

"What is it? What's happening?" they asked.

"What's happening?" repeated the Professor. "It worked—that's what's happening. We're inside the field of earth's gravity, and we're falling. Turn on the power again, Grimes, to brake the ship. We're going home!"

CHAPTER NINETEEN

Danny Delivers

The school bell rang.

"Class dismissed," said Miss Arnold. Then she added, "Danny Dunn and Joe Pearson, will you both stay for a moment after the others go?"

Danny and Joe glanced at each other and sighed. Their first day back in school had been rather hectic, with the other boys and girls constantly turning to point at them and whispering and passing notes. But it wasn't *their* fault.

It took longer than usual for the class to leave. "Snitcher" Philips came to ask Danny for his autograph, and Danny, who was used to this sort of thing after almost a month of it, wrote his name with a flourish. Finally everyone had gone, and Miss Arnold closed the classroom door and looked at the two space travelers.

"Well!" she said. "This has been quite a day. Sit down, boys."

They did so. Miss Arnold fixed her sharp eyes on them severely.

"In the first place," she said, "I'm glad to see

that you haven't changed too much. Danny, your arithmetic is certainly excellent now, but you must learn to pay more attention during Social Studies. And Joe—you'll *have* to stop writing poety during class time."

They opened their mouths to protest, but she held up her hand, smiling. "I'm not really going to scold you," she said. "I know how exciting it is to be home again. Why, you're both famous! You've been on radio and television programs, you've been in all the papers, and you have both met the President of the United States. It will be hard for you to settle down to school again after all that."

Danny cleared his throat. "Yes, ma'am," he said, "but we're going to do it. We're going to settle down."

"Good. Don't let your fame go to your heads. There will be other adventures. The whole world is open to you. I want you to remember that now you're preparing for the rest of your lives."

"I'm going to college," Danny said. "We made enough money out of magazine articles and appearances on TV so that my Mom doesn't have to worry any more about that. I'm going to be a scientist."

"That's fine. What about you, Joe?"

"Well . . ." Joe scratched his head. "I don't know. I'm sort of interested in science now, though I never used to be."

There was a tap at the door. Miss Arnold called, "Come in."

Professor Bullfinch entered. "Oh, sorry to bother you," he said. "I didn't know the boys would still be here."

"I can let them go now if you want them, Professor," said Miss Arnold.

"Oh, no. I wanted to see you. I thought I'd ask you how they had adjusted to their first day back in school."

"Very well indeed," Miss Arnold said. "It will take us a few days to get back to normal, I suppose."

"How's Dr. Grimes?" Danny asked. "Did he go back to Washington this morning?"

"Oh, yes. He got word that he has been elected President of the new Anti-gravity Space Travel Society," said Professor Bullfinch. "You know —that used to be the International Rocket Society. He said to tell you he'd send you new lapel pins when they're ready."

"Well," said Miss Arnold, "I think that's all, then. I hope, Dan, that you'll buckle down to Social Studies. And—I know it will be hard, but I do hope you've given up daydreaming in class for good."

"I have, Miss Arnold," Danny said earnestly. "I'm going to work hard so I can get to college. But that reminds me—"

He went to his desk and pulled out a brown manila envelope. From it he took a sheaf of paper.

"I brought this in this morning and meant to give it to you, but I forgot," he said.

"What is it?"

"Five hundred sentences," Danny said with a mischievous smile. "Don't you remember? 'Space flight is a hundred years away.'"

Miss Arnold turned pink. Then she said, "Oh."

"I wrote them during our flight," Danny explained. "Between Mars and Saturn."

"When on earth did you have time to write five hundred sentences?" the Professor asked. "Or perhaps I should say, 'when *off* earth.'"

"When I checked the supplies every day," Danny grinned. "I used to write a few sentences each time."

Professor Bullfinch snorted with amusement. Then he said, "You certainly are a determined boy. But Danny, how could you be so sure you'd get back again with your sentences?"

Danny smiled at him. "You were there, Professor," he replied. "I knew you'd find a way."

The Professor clapped him on the back. "Thank you, my boy," he said, "but it was *you* who found the way."

Danny blushed and was silent.

The Professor added, almost to himself, "Yes —you young people, you are the hope and future of science."

Miss Arnold, still holding the sentences, had a most peculiar expression on her face.

She said, "Danny, I'll keep these as a souvenir of you and of the first space flight. But there's one thing I'd like to ask you, and I'd like a frank answer. Did you do these just to—to get even with me because it was a kind of old-fashioned punishment?"

Danny turned to her. "Why, no! Gee, of course not, Miss Arnold. You gave me that assignment, and you told me that I shouldn't forget

The Professor clapped him on the back

to bring my work in to school, so I did them. I thought you'd be happy."

"I am. But you didn't get my message?"

"Your message? When?"

"On that Saturday morning when you and Joe began your trip. At about ten o'clock—"

"At ten we were just crawling under the barn, I guess."

"I see. Well it's—it's really too bad."

Miss Arnold suddenly bit her lip and became very red in the face.

"Your mother phoned me," she went on. "She explained that you had written the sentences but that Professor Bullfinch had carried them off by accident. She said you'd gone to try to get them back. So I told her you were excused. I said you needn't write the sentences again."

"What?" cried Danny. "I was excused?"

Miss Arnold couldn't hold in her laughter any longer and exploded. "Oh, dear," she gasped. "I'm so sorry, Dan. I just can't help it."

Both Joe and the Professor began to laugh too.

Danny stared from one to the other.

"Five hundred—" he said. "Oh—!"

Then he began to giggle too. And soon he was laughing louder than any of the others.

About the Authors and the Artist

JAY WILLIAMS is the author of five juveniles including *The Roman Moon Mystery,* which won a Boys' Club of America Award in 1949, and five adult books including *The Good Yeoman, The Rogue from Padua, The Siege,* and the highly regarded *A Change of Climate.* Born in Buffalo, New York, Mr. Williams was educated at the University of Pennsylvania, Columbia University, and the Art Students League. He was for several years in show business as an entertainer and stage manager and has been assistant press agent for the Group Theatre. He and his wife live in Redding, Connecticut, with their son Christopher and daughter Victoria.

RAYMOND ABRASHKIN is the author and co-producer of the very popular and successful *Little Fugitive,* which was named Best American Film at the 1954 Venice Film Festival. In addition to over fifty children's records, he has written the librettos for four children's operas. Born in Brooklyn in 1911, Mr. Abrashkin received his B.S. degree from City College of New York in 1931 and taught in the New York City Public Schools from 1931 to 1940. Following service in the U.S. Maritime Service, he was an editor at Reynal & Hitchcock, Inc., and since 1946 has devoted his full time to free-lance work. He now lives with his family which includes John, fifteen, and Hank, twelve, in Weston, Connecticut.

EZRA JACK KEATS has illustrated a number of books including Jay Williams' recent *A Change of Climate.* He was born and bred in Brooklyn and attended the Art Students League in New York City. Besides spending a year in Paris, his on-the-spot research for book illustrations has taken him to many different locations including Cuba and Scotland. Mr. Keats now lives in New York City.

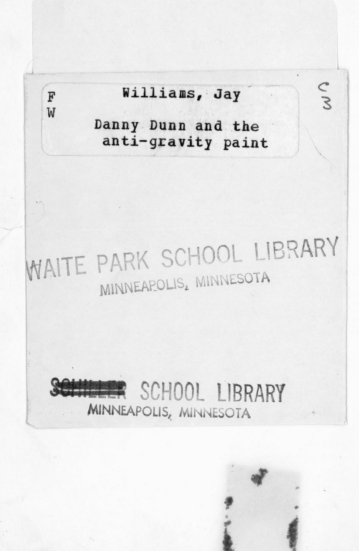